THE CASTLE OF FEAR

Tatika Lynch's exotic good looks first aroused the attentions of the lecherous Lord Crowley. Later, her wit and intelligence captivated him. He would possess her —at any cost. But Tatika did not love him and would not marry him.

Desperate and alone, she fled to Scotland. There she took refuge in Castle Craig with the Dowager Duchess and her son.

The Duke was young and extraordinarily handsome. Yet there was something hidden in his past, a dreadful secret people only whispered about.

How could anyone love such a man, Tatika wondered. Yet there was a strange magnetic quality about the Duke. Tatika found herself drawn to him more and more . . .

Books by BARBARA CARTLAND

Romantic Novels

The Fire of Love
The Unpredictable Bride
Love Holds the Cards
A Virgin in Paris
Love to the Rescue
Love Is Contraband
The Enchanting Evil
The Unknown Heart
The Secret Fear
The Reluctant Bride
The Pretty Horse-Breakers
The Audacious Adventuress
Lost Enchantment
Halo for the Devil

The Irresistible Buck
The Complacent Wife
The Odious Duke
The Daring Deception
No Darkness for Love
The Little Adventure
Lessons in Love
Journey to Paradise
The Bored Bridegroom
The Penniless Peer
The Dangerous Dandy
The Ruthless Rake
The Wicked Marquis
The Castle of Fear

Autobiographical and Biographical

The Isthmus Years 1919–1939
The Years of Opportunity 1939–1945
I Search for Rainbows 1945–1966
We Danced All Night 1919–1929
Ronald Cartland
 (with a Foreword by Sir Winston Churchill)
Polly, My Wonderful Mother

Historical

Bewitching Women
The Outrageous Queen
 (The Story of Queen Christina of Sweden)
The Scandalous Life of King Carol
The Private Life of King Charles II
The Private Life of Elizabeth, Empress of Austria
Josephine, Empress of France
Diane de Poitiers
Metternich—the Passionate Diplomat

Sociology

You in the Home
The Fascinating Forties
Marriage for Moderns
Be Vivid, Be Vital
Love, Life and Sex
Look Lovely, Be Lovely
Vitamins for Vitality
Husbands and Wives

Etiquette
The Many Facets of Love
Sex and the Teenager
The Book of Charm
Living Together
Woman—The Enigma
The Youth Secret
The Magic of Honey

Barbara Cartland's Health Food Cookery Book
Barbara Cartland's Book of Beauty and Health
Barbara Cartland's Book of Useless Information

The Castle of Fear

Barbara Cartland

BANTAM BOOKS · TORONTO · NEW YORK · LONDON

THE CASTLE OF FEAR
A Bantam Book published October 1974
2nd printing
3rd printing
4th printing

Bantam Books are published by Bantam Books, Inc. Its trade-
mark consisting of the words "Bantam Books" and the por-
trayal of a bantam, is registered in the United States Patent
office and in other countries. Marca Registrada. Bantam
Books, Inc., 666 Fifth Avenue, New York, New York 10019.

PRINTED IN THE UNITED STATES OF AMERICA

Dedicated to the lovely H.H. Princess Helena Moutafian whose ancestors, the Gagarins, were among the first Vikings to land on the shores of Russia.

Author's Note

The extraordinary achievements of the Scandinavian sea warriors—the Vikings—between A.D. 800 to 1050 depended primarily on their ships. It was therefore their custom to bury their dead in ships under huge burrows. These can still be seen in the North of Scotland.

And many inhabitants of Sutherland, Caithness, the Orkneys and Shetland have Scandinavian characters and names.

The great Eastern movement carried the Rus, as the Scandinavian's were called, into and around Novgorod and Kiev. Rurik was the first Knyaz—Prince of Novgorod in A.D. 862.

Chapter One

1886

The Peeresses, in their glittering tiaras swept to the ground in a deep curtsey as following a fanfare of trumpets the Royal Procession entered the Ball-room.

Tatika thought that with their full flounced skirts and bustles ending in a sweeping train, they looked like flowers blowing in the wind.

Something artistic within her thrilled to the beauty of the spectacle.

The Prince and Princess of Wales approached the Royal dais. There was a role of drums and the band played "God Save the Queen."

A State Ball at Buckingham Palace was naturally more glamorous and more exciting than the dozens of other Balls which Tatika had attended night after night during the London Season.

There was no doubt that not only the Ladies with their dazzling jewels lent an entrancing glitter to the proceedings, but the Gentlemen also added a splendour of their own.

There is nothing more attractive than a medal-bedecked uniform, the embroidered full-dress of an

1

Ambassador or the knee-breeches of Court dress when worn with the Order of the Garter.

The Princess of Wales was as usual the most beautiful woman present. In silver and white brocade, veiled with tulle looped with bunches of white ostrich feathers, she made all other women seem to pale into insignificance beside her.

"The Frenchman was right," Tatika thought, "who told me that England is a land of beautiful women!"

The Royal Procession which had been preceded by the Lord Chamberlain, the Lord Kenmare, had now dispersed.

The Ladies and the Gentlemen of the Household and other distinguished guests had followed the Prince and Princess of Wales onto the dance-floor, who had opened the Ball, and were moving elegantly and gracefully through the steps of the quadrille to the strains of a string band.

Tatika stood by her Step-mother, who was seated on the Ambassadress's red velvet bench.

She had not yet been asked to dance, but she knew that as soon as the initial formalities of the Ball were over, she would have any number of partners.

"The Marquis of Lorne is, I think, a very good-looking man," she heard the Ambassadress who was sitting next to her Step-mother say.

"Very distinguished," Lady Lynch agreed. "And I always admire the Earl of Fyfe. The Scots certainly stand out on occasions like this."

The Ambassadress laughed.

"The English will have to look to their laurels! But the competition is not so intense now that the Duke of Strathcraig no longer graces our Ball-rooms."

"I miss him," Lady Lynch said. "I have always thought he is one of the most handsome men I have ever seen."

"We all thought that!" the Ambassadress smiled. "It is a pity—a great pity—that he has decided to incarcerate himself in the North."

"You mean," Lady Lynch said, "that ever since the—the tragedy he has shunned society."

"I am told he will not even accept an invitation to Balmoral. In fact . . ."

The Ambassadress lowered her voice so that Tatika could not hear what was said.

She was not really paying attention; at the same time she could not help wondering who it was who could bring such a warmth of admiration to her Step-mother's voice.

Lady Lynch was notoriously critical and she usually had something disparaging to say about everyone.

A Gentleman resplendent in military uniform bowed to Tatika and asked if she would dance with him.

He was a young Guardsman who had pursued her for some time and she had hoped that she might have avoided him this evening. But as no-one else had invited her to take the floor, there was nothing she could do but agree.

"I must see you," he said intensely as soon as they were out of earshot of the chaperons.

"You saw me last night," Tatika answered, "and the night before."

"I mean alone."

"You know that is impossible!"

"Why should it be? There must be places where we can meet. You could tell your Step-mother you are going to the Library or the British Museum. Any excuse so that she would not be suspicious."

"And why should I do that?"

Tatika's voice was cold and the young man glanced at her anxiously before he said:

"You know the reason. I have told you over and over again that I love you."

"Just as I have told you a dozen times," Tatika said, "that I do not want to listen to you. In fact I will not do so!"

"Supposing I approach your father?"

"I am sure he would turn you away. Let me

make it quite clear, once and for all, I have no wish to marry you or ... anyone else for that matter."

"What is wrong with me? Why should you not love me? I cannot be all that replusive."

"I am sorry, Captain Witheringham," Tatika said firmly, "but there is no point in discussing it further."

"Then what am I to do?" he asked desperately.

"I have no idea," Tatika answered.

The dance came to an end as she spoke and she walked back towards her Step-mother.

Captain Witheringham followed her and stood uncomfortably beside the two women, making polite conversation until the music started again.

Tatika looked round the Ball-room at the massed flowers, the white and gold pillars, the Royal dais, the red velvet of the Duchesses' bench, the band playing in the gallery and the less distinguished guests standing behind a long red rope.

The Equerries, the Gentlemen of the Household, and in the corridors and on the stairs, the Gentlemen at Arms were all magnificently resplendent.

"This should be a setting for romance," she told herself but knew that as far as she was concerned it was interesting but certainly not romantic.

Another partner whom she did not know so well as Captain Witheringham claimed a dance and inevitably made the same sort of advances. She was as coldly indifferent as she had been to the young Guardsman.

It was only when she returned for the fifth time to her Step-mother's side that Lady Lynch said:

"After this dance, your father and I must join the Royal Procession for supper. Lady Carthew has promised to chaperon you and several other girls in our absence. Do not forget to go to her when the dance is over."

"No, Step-mama," Tatika answered.

Lady Lynch was not really listening for her answer. She was looking for her husband who, smart in his diplomatic uniform, was slowly edging his way through the crowd towards her.

In the confusion while the most distinguished guests arranged themselves to follow the Prince and Princess of Wales into the Gold Plate Room where supper was served, Tatika slipped away.

She had a feeling that, if she did not do so, Captain Witheringham would ask for another dance and she had no desire to discuss the same subject once again.

She left the State Ball-room and moving through a large Reception Room she found herself in an Ante-room.

She had been there earlier in the evening when Lady Lynch had accompanied her and one of her partners to look at a recently painted picture of the Queen with her grand-children.

She had not been particularly interested in the portrait, but she had noticed there was a French window open onto a balcony and she had a sudden wish to see the garden.

Now she moved across the room and out into the warm July night.

The garden, as she had expected, was lovely. There were tiny fairy lights in the trees, and as there was a pale moon rising up the sky it was easy to see the lawns, the terraces and a fountain playing in the distance.

Tatika drew in a deep breath.

As always when she felt that people were too oppressive and men too possessive, the beauty of nature gave her a feeling of happiness and contentment that no human being could do.

All this afternoon she had been occupied in calling on her Step-mother's friends, making conversation and answering desultory questions. Now for the first time she felt alone—free and as if able to breathe.

"There is nothing lovelier," she thought, "than a garden in the moon-light."

Especially this was true of the Royal Garden.

Her thoughts carried her away into a mystic world of her own and it was with a sudden start she came back to reality as a voice asked:

"What are you thinking about, pretty little lady, here alone?"

She turned quickly and saw standing just behind her a large man she had noticed earlier in the evening.

He had been looking at her in such a penetrating way as she waltzed by that she had wondered for a moment if she had met him. She then decided that he was in fact a stranger.

Now he was smoking a cigar which was an unforgivable breach of etiquette! Somehow the rich fragrance of tobacco jarred upon the sweet scent of the flowers rising from the garden.

Tatika did not answer, wondering what she should reply to someone who had not been introduced. Then the newcomer said:

"You are Tatika Lynch. I know your father and I also knew your Mother."

"You knew my Mother?"

Tatika's tone was eager.

"Yes indeed," he replied. "Perhaps I had better introduce myself: my name is Crowley—Lord Crowley."

"I have heard of you," Tatika answered, "Papa often speaks of your spectacular successes on the race course."

"I have some good horses," Lord Crowley said indifferently. "I have been wanting to meet you, Tatika."

She stiffened in surprise that he should use her Christian name so familiarly, before she asked:

"Because you knew my Mama?"

"She was very beautiful," Lord Crowley said, "and you are very like her."

"I have always hoped that I might be," Tatika replied. "I remember her as the loveliest person imaginable, but she died when I was ten."

There was something very wistful in her voice.

The moon-light on her face revealed the sadness in her large eyes which seemed too big for her small oval face.

There was no doubt that she was exquisite and very different in every way from the other young girls moving round the Ball-room.

There was something mysterious and very un-English about her face with its perfect features, the haunting depth of her eyes and the misty darkness of her hair.

Lord Crowley came a little nearer and lent against the balustrade of the balcony.

"I also knew your Grandfather," he said. "I stayed with him in Russia about eight years ago."

Tatika did not speak, she only looked at him, a question in her eyes.

"I spoke to him of your mother."

Tatika was very still, waiting.

"I thought perhaps her death would have softened the old autocrat," he went on, "but all Prince Kaupenski said was—'My daughter? I never had one'."

Tatika drew in a deep breath.

"I have always hoped ever since I was a child that one day I would meet my Russian relations."

"The Prince is now dead," Lord Crowley said, "but there must be a number of aunts and uncles, cousins of one sort or another, who would welcome you."

"I doubt it," Tatika answered, "and anyway I shall never forgive them for the way they treated Mama."

"My dear, she ran away with your father!"

"Was that such a crime?" Tatika asked hotly. "They were in love! Surely the Russians are emotional enough to understand love?"

"And you—do you understand it?"

Lord Crowley's voice had a new note which made Tatika look at him sharply.

He must be over forty, she thought, and he

might once have been passably good-looking, but now he was florid and over-weight.

Then from long experience she recognised the look in his eyes and turned her head away towards the garden.

"Tell me more about my mother," she said quietly.

"I would rather talk about you. How old are you, Tatika?"

"I am over eighteen," Tatika replied. "I should have come out last year, but my Grandmother, Papa's mother, died in April and we were therefore in deep mourning."

"So you are a somewhat belated debutante? Yet still the loveliest that any man could imagine."

"You are very kind," Tatika answered politely but her voice was cold. "And now I must return to the Ball-room. I should not have left it, had it not been so hot."

"There is no hurry," Lord Crowley said. "Your father and Step-mother are in the Royal Procession; I saw them going down to supper."

"And surely that is where you, My Lord, should be."

"I wished to talk to you."

"So you followed me?"

"Yes. I saw you escape and, pleading a sudden indisposition, I left the Lady I should have escorted alone and disconsolate all on your behalf."

"I think that was unnecessary and unkind," Tatika said. "Perhaps she will go hungry."

"I am sure an efficient and watchful Equerry will take my place," Lord Crowley said. "But as I have given up my supper for you, you could at least be gracious enough to entertain me."

Tatika was silent. She knew now that she did not like this large, rather over-powering man. There was something about him which made her secretly afraid.

She was never wrong in her impressions of people.

She would know, almost as soon as she met someone, what they were like, whether she could trust them, or whether after a first acquaintance she must do her best to avoid them.

Her instinct, she thought, came from long practice gained in wandering over Europe at her father's heels moving from diplomatic post to diplomatic post, from country to country.

Her education may have been neglected in many ways, but certainly not where people were concerned and especially men.

"You are very beautiful," Lord Crowley said quietly, but he looked at her, Tatika thought, as if he were appraising a horse. "Are you in love?"

The question was so unexpected that it shocked her.

"No, certainly not!" she said sharply.

"And yet you speak as if you understand that exciting, that elusive emotion which we all seek in one way or another."

"I have never been in love."

"And yet you long for it," Lord Crowley said. "What woman does not wish to be swept off her feet, to find the Prince Charming of her dreams, and of course live happily ever after?"

There was a touch of sarcasm in his voice and involuntarily, without thinking, Tatika asked:

"You are married, My Lord?"

"I have been married," he corrected. "I have been a widower now for nearly five years."

"I am sorry."

"There is no need to offer me your condolences," he said. "I do not miss my wife, we had very little in common with each other."

Tatika looked at him in surprise.

"Then why did you marry her?" she asked.

Then, even as she spoke, she realised it was not only an impertinent question, but too intimate a one.

"I apologise," she exclaimed quickly before he

could answer. "I should not have said that. And now, My Lord, I must return to the Ball-room."

She made a movement towards the window but he reached out and took her hand in his.

"I want you to stay here with me," he said, "I want to talk to you, Tatika, and more than anything else I want to kiss you."

She tried to pull her hand away from him, but he would not release it. He attempted to put his arm round her, but she retreated away from him further down the balcony.

"Kindly let me go."

Her voice was controlled and cold. It was a tone which invariably put a younger man in his place if he dared to attempt anything so familiar as touching her.

Lord Crowley merely laughed.

"There speaks the imperious Russian blood! I can see, little Tatika, that you should be cracking your whip over the serfs who cringe at your feet, or driving your sleigh at a head-long pace over the snows."

His voice deepened as he went on:

"There is nothing lifeless and frigid about you, and that is why I want to kiss your lips and feel the fire in them."

"How dare you speak to me like this!" Tatika stormed. "You know you have no right!"

"And how will you prevent me?"

He challenged her boldly and she felt a little tremor of fear before she replied proudly:

"I do not think my father would tolerate my being insulted, especially by someone who calls himself his friend."

"And do you really think your father would believe I was insulting you?" Lord Crowley asked, and she hated the sarcastic note in his voice and the smile on his lips.

"I wish to go back to the Ball-room. Please let me pass."

She wrenched her hand from his as she spoke and looked up at him defiantly.

For a moment she thought he would refuse, then he seemed to change his mind.

"Very well," he said, "I will take you back and I will dance with you. I wish to hold you in my arms."

"I will not dance with you," Tatika declared.

But as she walked ahead of him through the Reception Room, she was vividly conscious of him walking beside her, of his imperturbability and his quite obvious confidence that she would do as he wished.

They reached the Ball-room, a dance was in progress, and before she could escape, Lord Crowley's arm was round her waist.

She made herself rigid, hoping her dislike would communicate itself to him without resorting to words. But as they danced she was aware that he was watching her with a dangerous glint in his eyes and that her silence did not upset him in the slightest.

He danced well, which she had not expected and, because she moved always with an exquisite grace, it was difficult to be as stiff and unbending as she wished to be, even while she resented the feel of his hand against her back.

"When can I see you again? Tomorrow?"

"I am busy," Tatika replied briefly.

"I will take you driving in the park."

"I cannot accept your invitation."

Her voice was sarcastic and he laughed softly.

"Are you really trying to refuse my attentions?"

He had goaded her into a reply.

"Shall I make it very clear, Lord Crowley?" she asked. "I must thank you for your invitation, but I have no intention of accepting it tomorrow or any other day."

"Do you know," he asked, "that your eyes seem to flash like fire when you are angry? I never knew a woman could be so alluring when she is incensed. Usually their faces are ugly at such times. Yours is even more beautiful than it is in repose!"

"I have no wish for your flattery."

"It is not flattery," he answered, "it is fact."

As he spoke the music ceased.

"Will you dance with me again?" he enquired.

"I think you know the answer to that," Tatika replied.

He laughed as if she had said something amusing.

"You are very young," he said, "but I still want to kiss you."

For a moment she looked at him furiously, then she turned and walked away to where she saw Lady Carthew was sitting.

Driving back from Buckingham Palace, Lady Lynch yawned then said:

"It was very hot! All the same I think it was one of the best Balls we have ever been to at Buckingham Palace. What did you think, Dominic?"

"I enjoyed it," Sir Dominic replied.

He put out his hand as he spoke to touch his daughter who was sitting opposite them on the small seat with her back to the horses.

"Did you enjoy yourself, Tatika?" he asked. "A great number of people congratulated me on your good looks."

"It was a very splendid sight," Tatika answered.

"I saw that you danced every dance," her father said. "Who took you down to supper?"

"I did not want any," Tatika replied. "Several of my partners suggested escorting me to the Supper-room, but I preferred to dance."

"When I was a girl," Lady Lynch said, "I found a flirtation was so much easier when one had a glass of wine in one's hand and delicious food to eat."

Sir Dominic laughed.

"Nonsense, Elaine! I remember when we first met in Vienna, we sat out every dance in the garden and caused a tremendous flutter in the dovecot."

"That is true," Lady Lynch said," "but you were very persuasive, Dominic."

"I think it was you who persuaded me," he replied.

Tatika was sure that was true. From the very moment her Step-mother had set eyes on her father, she had been determined to marry him.

He had resisted the blandishments of so many women that at first she had not been alarmed.

But then she had realised that there was a steely determination behind that pretty if somewhat vacant face, which enabled the gay young widow to cling to and entwine herself round a man so that it was impossible for him to escape.

Sir Dominic had not escaped, and Tatika at sixteen, after years of having her father to herself, had to compete with a rival for his affections.

"I have told the coachman to drop me at White's," Sir Dominic said as they drove up St. James's Street.

"You are not going to be late are you, Dominic?" Lady Lynch asked sharply.

"No," he answered, "but I promised I would look in at a party that Freddy is giving. I expect the stakes will be pretty high by this time."

"Then do not gamble," Lady Lynch admonished him. "You know we cannot afford it!"

"No-one knows that better than I do," Sir Dominic answered with a touch of bitterness in his voice.

The carriage came to a standstill and he bent forward to kiss Tatika's cheek.

"Good night, my dear," he said.

She watched him cross the pavement to his Club. There was no doubt that although he was getting on for sixty Sir Dominic was still a handsome and attractive man.

A footman shut the door and climbed up on the box.

"Your father is worried about money," Lady Lynch said as the horses started up.

"That is nothing new," Tatika answered lightly.

"Then, if you realise his difficulties, I cannot imagine why you do not do something about it."

Tatika did not speak and her Step-mother went on:

"Your father has been, in my opinion, over-generous to you. He has spent a great deal of money on giving you a season in London, money he can ill afford. It is now the 19th of July and as far as I can see all the expense has been wasted."

"You mean," Tatika said slowly, "because I am not engaged to be married."

"Well surely out of the large number of men who pay you attention you could find one to please your ultra-fastidious taste."

Lady Lynch's tone was scathing, and the colour came into Tatika's cheeks as she replied.

"I am sorry, Step-mama, but I am not in love with any of the men whom I have met in the last two months."

"In love!" Lady Lynch said scathingly. "Who is asking you to be in love? What we want you to do, Tatika, is to get married to someone who is rich and can offer you a decent position as his wife. As far as I can see there are quite a number of men who qualify under that heading."

Tatika did not reply and she continued:

"I am well aware that it is your behaviour which is preventing them from approaching your father. I am not a fool, Tatika! You may bamboozle him, but you do not bamboozle me. You are cold and the manner in which you refuse a man almost before he has the time to ask you to be his wife is causing talk."

"What do you mean by that?" Tatika asked.

"Lady Heron was telling me tonight how unhappy you have made her son. He told his mother that you had slapped him down almost before the words reached his lips."

"You could hardly expect me to marry Lord Heron!" Tatika exclaimed. "He is subject to fits and appears to me to be half-witted."

"He has a big estate in Wiltshire and the Herons are an old family," Lady Lynch retorted.

Tatika looked at her with wide eyes.

"Are you seriously suggesting I should accept Lord Heron?"

"I am seriously suggesting it would be quite a good match for a girl without a dowry, who is increasingly an encumbrance upon her father and—his wife."

"I am sure Papa would not wish it."

"Your father will wish what I tell him to wish—that you should be settled," Lady Lynch snapped. "If you think I desire to cart around a débutante when I myself am only thirty-four, you must be demented."

They both knew she had passed her thirty-eighth birthday, but it was not the moment to be precise over details.

"It was not my idea that I should have a season," Tatika said after a moment. "I was quite content to keep in the background, to go on with my studies."

"And where will that get you," Lady Lynch interposed, "unless you intend to marry the man who hands out the books in the lending library? Do not be so ridiculous, Tatika! Your father is greatly respected in diplomatic circles. Naturally he wants his daughter to marry well. And as far as I am concerned, the sooner the better."

"You have made that very obvious before."

"What I say does not seem to sink into your head," Lady Lynch said angrily. "But I wish to make it very clear to you, Tatika, that you cannot go on behaving as you are now—keeping men at arm's length, preventing them from paying their addresses to you, and quite obviously forbidding them to approach your father."

"What is the point of their talking to Papa, if I have no intention of marrying them?" Tatika enquired.

Lady Lynch made an exclamation of annoyance.

"As I have already said, there are two weeks left

before the end of the season," she remarked. "Already some people are leaving London. If you have not found a husband in that time I shall consider you a grossly ungrateful and selfish girl who has no feeling for her Father.

"He cannot afford to go on dressing you and keeping you when we hardly have enough money to live as it is."

Tatika sighed. She knew it was not only greed which prompted her Step-mother to make scenes like this, but also jealousy. She grudged every penny that her father spent on her.

It was true they had very little money. Diplomatic salaries were not high and Sir Dominic had always lived beyond his means.

It had been different before he was married. She and her father had somehow managed to be comfortable in the various capitals where they had lived after her mother's death.

But the new Lady Lynch required so much for herself. The money she spent on her clothes was astronomical, and she was, Tatika knew, always badgering her father for more jewels.

Her carriages and horses too had to be smarter than those of any other diplomat's wife, and she had a passion for entertaining.

It had been easy before her father was married for him to be entertained—as guest rather than host. But now he had to foot the bills and they were high.

"Have you listened to what I have been saying?" Lady Lynch asked as Tatika did not speak. "You have two weeks, Tatika, and if you have not found a husband in that time, whether you like it or not, I shall tell Lady Heron that you have changed your mind and that you accept her half-witted son."

"I will not marry Lord Heron," Tatika declared.

"Very well, choose yourself another husband," Lady Lynch said indifferently. "But I can promise you, one way or another, that you will be married before Christmas."

Tatika had no chance to reply because they now drew up outside the house in Charles Street which Sir Dominic had rented for the season.

He was between assignments at the moment having finished his appointment as Ambassador in Vienna and believed that on the retirement of the British Ambassador to Paris he would be offered the post.

In the meantime he was on leave, and the cheapest way to spend it would have been to live in the Elizabethan Manor House in Hertfordshire which had been in the possession of the Lynch family for over three hundred years.

But it was important that Tatika should make her "début" as she had been prevented from doing it the year before, and Lady Lynch had certainly not been reluctant to enjoy the gaieties of a London season.

Nevertheless it all involved a considerable expense, and as Tatika followed her Step-mother into the hall of the rented house, she thought with a sudden constriction of her heart that her father was undoubtedly in debt and there was, as far as she could see, only one prospect of his debts ever being paid.

"I have added to his debts," she thought, "yet even to help Papa, how can I marry someone I do not love?"

She thought as she spoke of the vacant face of Lord Heron and then almost in spite of herself she saw all too clearly the expression in Lord Crowley's eyes.

It was a glint that she knew all too well preluded uncomfortable situations, protestations and eventually recriminations.

At the thought of him she felt herself shiver.

"There is something horrid about him," she thought, "something which makes me feel afraid!"

Chapter Two

Tatika lay awake for a long time thinking of what her Step-mother had said.

She went over in her mind the men who she knew would be ready to ask for her hand in marriage should she give them the slightest encouragement.

Unfortunately there was not one that she felt she could consider as a husband, and she wondered despondently if she would ever find a man to whom she could give her heart.

Ever since her mother had died and she had lived with her father abroad, Tatika had been pursued by men.

There had always been older men who had tried to kiss her, younger men who had flirted with her, and as soon as she was grown up men who wished to marry her.

Something fastidious and very discriminating in her nature made her hate the thought of being touched by a man for whom she had no real affection.

It had been hard at times to restrain those who admired her beauty, and even her coldness was a challenge. But Tatika had learned, as her Step-mother had said, to check a man's interest almost before he himself was aware of it.

She thought sometimes she had second sight: she

would know as soon as she met a man if he was likely to be a problem.

It was not only the glint in his eyes or what he said, it was something Tatika felt reaching out invisibly towards her, something which made her shrink away from him as if he were a snake.

She wished to keep herself apart, she wished to continue, as one suitor had described her bitterly, as "an Ice Maiden freezing all those who come in contact with you."

"Shall I ever fall in love?" Tatika had asked herself despairingly at times.

Yet in her secret heart she was sure that one day she would find a man whom she would love and to whom she would be drawn irresistibly.

She knew that at times her Russian blood made her feel wild and unrestrained, and gave her strange longings and deep desires to which she was too innocent to put a name.

But they were there! Hidden beneath the surface, part of her dreams, part of her hope that some day she would love and be loved.

She did not know quite what she wanted of this imaginary lover. She only knew that some day, somewhere, somehow, she would meet him and would find in him the fulfillment of all she could not put into words.

"What am I to do?" she asked when she awoke in the morning.

She had not slept well and her dreams had been troubled. She knew it was because her Step-mother had said so positively that she had to be married before Christmas.

Everything in Tatika's life had changed from the moment that her father had re-married.

An extremely attractive man, Sir Dominic had found it impossible to live without the companionship and the affection of women. It had not been long after her mother's death before he had sought the consolation of soft sympathetic lips and loving hands.

Tatika had not been shocked; she had known how it was contrary to his nature for her father to be alone. She was also aware that in his own way he was desperately unhappy at the loss of his wife.

She had not been too young to realise how ecstatically happy her father and mother were.

The first ten years of her life seemed always in retrospection to have a golden glow about them; her mother had exuded happiness almost as if she moved in an aura of perpetual sunshine.

They had met when Dominic Lynch was a First Secretary at the British Embassy at St. Petersburg.

He had been thirty-eight, a gay, much sought after bachelor who found the beautiful women at the Czar's court an irresistible attraction.

Then quite unexpectedly, because young girls were seldom asked to the parties he attended every night, he had met the daughter of His Serene Highness Prince Kaupenski.

Katrina had been only seventeen, but in many ways she was far older than a girl of the same age would have been in England.

She and Dominic Lynch—he had not yet been Knighted in those days—looked into each other's eyes and as her mother had told Tatika when she was old enough to understand:

"We fell madly, irrevocably in love."

Even to hear her mother say the words was to convey to Tatika some of the ecstasy, the wonder and the passion that this girl and man with so much difference in their ages had felt for each other.

They both had been swept off their feet, and when the Prince had categorically refused even to discuss the marriage of his daughter with an unimportant Diplomat, they had run away together.

It was an act which could have ruined Dominic Lynch's career. In fact a protest from the Prince, or even more from the Czar, to the British Foreign Office would have had very serious repercussions.

But the Prince had merely cut his daughter out

of his life and insisted that none of her family or relatives should ever speak of her again.

That Katrina was therefore friendless, and penniless had not mattered to Dominic Lynch. He was far too happy.

But Tatika looking back felt that sometimes her mother must have been lonely; for she was wholeheartedly Russian and had little in common with people of other countries.

She was always charming, always beautiful. Her parties that she gave with her husband were invariably a success, but she always remained in her own heart an exile.

It was perhaps this inner isolation that she communicated to her daughter.

On her mother's death, it seemed to Tatika that she grew up over-night. She was still only a child and yet she no longer thought like one. She understood her father's misery and the way he could assuage his sorrow only with other women.

She managed in quite a remarkable way to keep his household running smoothly, to prevent his worrying over tiresome domestic details, to organise her own life so that he was not troubled by her.

It was Tatika who engaged her own teachers, it was Tatika who decided what she should learn, who chose her own clothes, and even engaged a governess as a chaperon.

She might, when she was sixteen, with poise and assurance easily have been a self-confident woman of thirty.

It was then the blow came! Sir Dominic succumbed to the blandishments and the determination of the young widow who had been pursuing him for over two years.

"I am to be married, Tatika," he told his daughter.

Tatika had stared at him with her large dark eyes and for a moment she did not speak.

"To Mrs. Winslow, Papa?"

"Who else?" Sir Dominic had enquired.

"Are you wise?"

It was a strange question for a daughter to ask her Father.

Sir Dominic had walked across the room to stand with his back to Tatika looking out over the garden of the British Embassy in Vienna.

"It has been pointed out to me for a long time that an Ambassador needs a wife," he said, "and Elaine, as you well know, will make an excellent Ambassadress."

Tatika said nothing. Sir Dominic turned from the window.

"It was inevitable and she is excessively fond of me."

There was no doubt from his tone that he was trying to excuse himself.

"If it will make you happy, Papa," Tatika said quietly.

"Happy! What is happiness?" Sir Dominic asked. "I do not think I have ever been happy since I lost your mother. But one has to go on living and my career is important."

"Of course it is, Papa. I hope that your marriage will be everything you expect it to be."

Tatika had spoken very quietly and then she had gone from the room closing the door behind her. She had known without being told that this was the end of a chapter in her life, and she was afraid of what the future might hold.

Lady Lynch made it very clear, as soon as she was safely married to Sir Dominic, that she disliked having a Step-daughter and found her an encumbrance in the house.

Because she knew she was unwanted, Tatika spent all the time she could studying languages, art and music outside the Embassy.

Even so, there were hard words when the bills came in and endless discourses on how much men dislike having a clever wife.

Tatika had long ceased to argue with her Step-mother and now watching the sunlight coming between the curtains over her window, she asked herself:

"Could it not be worse for a clever woman to endure a stupid husband?"

She thought of Lord Heron and shuddered! How could she possibly look at that vacant face across a table day after day or listen to the inanity of his conversation.

Even Captain Witheringham, who had no conversation outside Regimental gossip, would be preferable. But he was not in the running because, as Tatika well knew, he had no money with which to keep a wife.

"What do I want in a man?" she asked herself, and feeling restless rose from her bed although she had not yet been called, and drew back the curtains from her window.

She looked out blindly into the sunshine seeing not the tall houses on the other side of the road, but the faces of men she knew.

Handsome faces, well-bred ones, greedy, stupid, sharp, lustful! Faces, dozens of faces, and yet all of them had, she felt, nothing to offer her, nothing which aroused her interest or even, except out of politeness, her attention.

"What is wrong with me?" she wondered.

She came down early to breakfast, knowing that her father would not appear for another half-hour and her Step-mother would doubtless have breakfast in bed.

As she descended the stairs there was the sound of a knock and she saw the footman struggling into his silver-buttoned livery coat, cross the marble floor beneath her and open the door.

She saw him take something from a man outside, and as she reached the hall he said:

"These flowers are for you, Miss Tatika, with a note. The groom says he is to wait for an answer."

Tatika glanced at the flowers indifferently. She was used to receiving bouquets after a Ball or a party, but these she noticed were rather more expensive than those she usually received.

A profusion of white orchids were tastefully arranged in a basket and she wondered how they could have arrived so quickly since it was unlikely that shops were open at such an early hour.

She opened the note, not particularly interested in what it might contain. There was a coronet at the top of the writing-paper and she read:

> Will you drive with me in the Park, beautiful little Tatika? I could call for you at twelve o'clock. These flowers have just arrived from the country and they reminded me of you.

> Crowley

Tatika folded over the sheet of writing-paper. Then she said to the footman who was waiting:

"Tell the groom to inform his Master that Miss Lynch has another engagement."

"Very good, Miss."

The footman went towards the front door and Tatika walked into the Morning-Room and, tearing Lord Crowley's note into very small pieces, put them in the wastepaper-basket.

She hoped that her Step-mother would not learn of the invitation.

From long experience she was sure that Lord Crowley's interest in her was not serious. He was beguiled by her face, and like many older men before him he thought it amusing to flirt with a pretty young girl.

There had been a number of elderly Don Juan's of Lord Crowley's type in the years of Tatika's growing up. The men who were entertained at her father's Embassy were usually distinguished and therefore not in their first youth. The majority of them were married.

But that did not prevent them from pursuing, at times quite ardently, the daughter of their host and needing, as Tatika found, to be kept "at arm's length" from the first moment of their acquaintance.

"Lord Crowley is another aging Casanova," she thought with a little curl of her lips.

Apart from anything else she positively disliked him. There was something about the manner in which he had approached her and the look in his eyes which she had found repulsive.

She knew her worst fault was her strong feeling of dislike for some people and the manner in which at times she would find it almost impossible even to be ordinarily polite.

"I hope I never see him again!" she thought.

Why should she worry? It would be easy to refuse his invitations and she was not likely to encounter him at any of the Balls she attended at the very end of the season.

Her father had already said that he did not intend to go to Goodwood this year.

"Forget Lord Crowley," Tatika told herself.

However she wondered why the expression in his eyes as she had walked away from him in the Ballroom at Buckingham Palace had remained so vivid in her mind.

She had forgotten the flowers until later in the morning when Lady Lynch came into the Morning-room where Tatika was writing a number of letters of thanks to her various hostesses of previous evenings.

"Who sent those flowers in the hall?" Lady Lynch asked.

Tatika rose from the desk.

"Good morning, Step-mama."

"It is not a good morning as far as I am concerned," Lady Lynch replied sharply. "I have a head-

ache and Heaven knows what I shall feel like after the
Ball tonight. But of course you must go, and I must
sacrifice my health to chaperon you."

Tatika did not reply. She knew it was really her
Step-mother who was looking forward to the Ball,
and the fact that she must act as a chaperon was only
an excuse to grumble and make herself out to be a
martyr.

"I asked you who sent those flowers," Lady
Lunch said as Tatika did not speak.

"A man I danced with last night," Tatika replied
indifferently. "I had never met him before, and I cannot imagine why he should be so extravagant."

"Who was he?" Lady Lynch enquired. "Is he
single?"

"I heard that he had a wife," Tatika answered.

It was partially the truth and Lady Lynch
shrugged her shoulders to say petulantly.

"Married men will get you nowhere! Do not forget what I told you last night."

She walked from the room as she spoke and Tatika with a little sigh sat down again at her desk.

As soon as she had finished her letters, she went
to her bed-room to find, waiting for her, the old maid
who had been with her mother when she was a girl.

It had been fashionable for the Ladies of the
Czar's Court to have a French or English lady's maid.
Ellen had travelled to St. Petersburg, and when her
mistress had left with Sir Dominic she had gone with
her.

"Let us go out, Ellen dear," Tatika said, "I must
have some air."

"I thought you might feel like that, Miss Tatika,"
Ellen answered.

She was an elderly woman with a sweet expression, and apart from her father she was the only person that Tatika loved.

Looking at her little face now framed by her
dark hair, Ellen asked anxiously:

"What's worrying you? Has she been disagreeable again?"

There was no need to explain who "she" was.

"Her Ladyship has told me I must be married before Christmas."

"Don't you pay any attention to her," Ellen said crossly. "She's been trying to get you out ever since she married your father. It isn't right, and if she makes things too difficult you must speak to him."

"And what can Papa do?" Tatika asked. "He gives in to her Ladyship because he dislikes scenes."

She gave a little sigh.

"Oh, Ellen, if only you and I could go away and live somewhere in the country! Even the tiniest cottage would do for us. I am sure I could make a little money by writing or perhaps translating books, and we would be away from all this bickering and fault-finding."

"It's not right, Miss Tatika, that you should shut yourself away from the social world to which you belong," Ellen said firmly. "You've got to have your chance to meet nice people—to make friends."

Tatika smiled.

"Whenever I make friends, Papa is always posted somewhere else. Do you remember that charmnig family in Rome? I used to love being with them. But of course I have never seen them again."

"You are older now," Ellen said, "and perhaps you'll find someone fine and noble to love you as you should be loved."

Tatika gave a little laugh which had no humour in it.

"You are as bad as Step-mama, always talking about marriage."

"And what other life is there for a young Lady like yourself?" Ellen enquired. "You know as well as I do that your mother would have wanted you to marry as she did."

"That is exactly what I am prepared to do," Tatika answered, "when I fall in love."

"And there is no-one?" Ellen asked.

It was a question she had often asked before.

"No-one, Ellen, as you well know," Tatika replied.

She walked across the room.

"I asked myself when I got out of bed this morning, what is wrong with me. Why can I not fall in love with any of the men who approach me? But, Ellen, they are all either so ordinary, so dull—or else I positively hate them."

"It's a question of time," Ellen said consolingly. "Your mother fell in love at seventeen, but that was different. I shall never forget her saying to me, 'I love him, Ellen! I love him! I love him! And if Papa will not let us marry, then I shall run away with him!'"

This was a story Tatika had heard over and over again. It never failed to move her, and there always was that little throb in Ellen's voice as if her mother's ecstatic voice still echoed down the years.

"When I feel like that I will marry," Tatika said. "But until then I will not be coerced or brow-beaten, whatever Step-mama says."

"That's right, dearie. Don't you let her bully you," Ellen said. "But she'll try—you know she'll try."

"Yes, I know that," Tatika said solemnly then added: "Come on, Ellen, let us get out of the house. I want to go to the Library."

The rest of the day Tatika managed to keep out of her Step-mother's way. Fortunately Lady Lynch was out to luncheon, and as she felt tired she did not drag Tatika round in her carriage visiting friends as she had done on so many previous afternoons.

Instead Tatika was able to curl up on the sofa with a book, and after a time, because she was tired after so many late nights, she fell asleep.

She could not have slept for long when she awoke suddenly with an intense feeling of happiness.

Her dream was fading and yet she knew she had not been alone, someone had been with her, someone who had brought her happiness—a happiness which had seemed to envelop them both with a golden haze.

"I am happy," she whispered to herself.

Then she opened her eyes and found she was lying on the sofa, a book open on her lap.

"If only I could feel that in real life," she thought, and with the happiness in her dream still vivid, she went up to dress for dinner humming a little tune to herself.

The dinner-party was very much the same as all the other dinner-parties she had attended during the season.

There were huge tables decorated with smilax and loaded with enormous silver ornaments and candelabra holding lighted candles.

The hostess glittered in a high tiara and was festooned with necklaces, brooches, bracelets and rings of diamonds and pearls.

There was course after course of exotic rich food, of which Tatika ate very little, and her dinner partners were, she thought, almost identical with those of the night before and the night before that.

One was a Guardsman who described to her in some detail the Army Manoeuvres in which he had taken part on Salisbury Plain.

On the other side was a chinless young Peer whose only interest as far as Tatika could discover was in driving a tandem rather faster and more dangerously than any of his contemporaries.

Neither of them ever read a book and their political knowledge was confined to repeating rather stupid stories about the Radicals which Tatika had heard several times already.

She found herself wondering if anyone really enjoyed parties of this sort.

The hostess's daughter was a shy rather plain girl, dressed unbecomingly in bunched white tulle which showed her figure to a disadvantage, and squeezed into too tight white satin slippers and even tighter white kid gloves.

It was obvious she had nothing to say and was too shy to respond to the few attempts her dinner partners made at drawing her into the conversation.

Tatika was quite certain that when they reached the dance she would spend most of the evening by her mother's side or hide herself pathetically in the Ladies' Cloak-room.

The girls of course only played a small part in the evening's entertainment.

Every hostess, if she gave a Ball, entertained her own friends, and Tatika saw the same be-jewelled nobility appearing at all the Season's Balls, afraid that if they were not present their friends would think they had not been invited.

When the long-drawn-out dinner was over the Ladies withdrew upstairs.

There was the same chatter amongst the younger girls of how many parties they had been to and how many were left, the same whispered gossip amongst their mothers with invariably a spiteful note in their voices as they disparaged or slandered one of their friends.

"At least," Tatika told herself, "the parties at the Embassies were a dozen times more interesting than this."

There her father had entertained Statesmen and politicians, Diplomats from other countries, and the conversation had been intelligent if often stereotyped.

"In contrast this is almost too boring to be endurable," Tatika thought.

She wandered away from a group of girls of her own age and saw apprehensively that her Step-mother was talking to Lady Heron.

There was something in the way that their heads were nodding and their voices were lowered which told Tatika they were talking about her.

Her lips tightened.

"I will not marry Lord Heron!" she vowed.

It was with a sense of relief that she realised that their hostess was making a move, and the party went downstairs with a flutter of silk, tulle and gauze, their shoulders covered in wraps of velvet and taffeta, swansdown and fur.

The Ball was taking place in Park Lane at one of the huge houses at the back of which there was a large garden.

It was hot and stifling in the Ball-room and Tatika welcomed a suggestion from her partner that they should move outside.

The garden was inevitably lit with Chinese lanterns and fairy lights. Tatika and the young Secretary from the Austrian Embassy who was escorting her had just reached the lawn when she saw with a sense of dismay a tall man walking towards them whom she recognised immediately.

She would have turned aside but she was too late.

"Good evening, Tatika," Lord Crowley said.

Tatika dropped him a small curtsey and made no effort to reply.

"I do not think we have met," Lord Crowley said to her escort.

"My name is Windischgretz, My Lord. I had the good fortune to back your horse in the Gold Cup at Ascot."

"I am glad to hear that," Lord Crowley said. "Put a little on the animal I am running in the Goodwood Stakes, I think he has a chance."

"I thank Your Lordship," the Austrian said gratefully.

"And now perhaps you will be so obliging as to relinquish your partner into my keeping," Lord Crowley said. "I have something rather important to discuss with Miss Lynch. I hope she will be able to give you another dance later in the evening."

"I naturally cannot refuse your request, My Lord," the young man said politely.

He bowed to Tatika, then to Lord Crowley, and moved away towards the house.

"That was quite unnecessary," Tatika exclaimed, "and very high-handed!"

"I have to be high-handed where you are concerned," Lord Crowley replied. "Why did you refuse to come driving with me today?"

"I had another engagement."

"I doubt if it was a very important one," he said, "and as I have gone to a great deal of trouble to cancel my other arrangements for this evening so I could meet you at this extremely dull function, I hope you will reward me."

"I did not invite you to come here."

"I should hope not," Lord Crowley replied. "It is the type of entertainment I go out of my way to avoid."

"Then why come?" Tatika asked. "You are well aware, My Lord, that I did not wish to see you."

"You are very frank. Shall we sit down?"

"I think I must return to the Ball-room."

He gave a little laugh.

"I have no intention of allowing you to do that, and if you insist I have the feeling it will be an unconventional tug-of-war. I have out-manoeuvered you, Tatika, so give in with a good grace. Come and sit where we can talk."

Feeling that he might in fact forcibly prevent her from leaving him, Tatika holding her head high moved a little way onto the lawn. There were chairs set under the trees and in arbours behind well filled flower beds.

She would have chosen a chair under a tree, but Lord Crowley walked purposefully towards one of the arbours, and because she did not wish to make a scene Tatika followed him.

The cushioned seat was not in darkness as there were fairy lights leading up to it and a large yellow Chinese lantern hung on the branch of an adjacent bough.

Seating herself as far from Lord Crowley as possible, Tatika turned her face away from him and said coldly:

"I must not stay long, as Your Lordship well knows. What is it you wish to say to me?"

"Shall I tell you you are the most beautiful person I have ever seen?" Lord Crowley enquired.

"That would not be true," Tatika answered, "and I have no desire to hear you say it."

"As a matter of fact it is true," he replied. "I thought when I saw you last night that I must have stepped back through the years and was watching your mother move round the dance-floor at the Embassy in Rome. She had a grace that was indescribable and you have it too."

Tatika did not speak. She wanted to hear about her mother. She longed to talk about her. But something within her told her this man was dangerous and she must not on any account encourage him.

"I admired your mother," Lord Crowley went on, "and like a great many other men I would have been only too willing to lay my heart at her feet if she would have even noticed it was there. But as I am sure you know, she had eyes for no-one but your father."

"That is true," Tatika said softly, "they were in love."

"A love few people are privileged to enjoy," Lord Crowley said. "You tell me that you have not yet lost your heart to a man, little Tatika, so why not give it to me?"

Tatika stiffened. Her thoughts had been with her mother and now she heard a note in Lord Crowley's voice that she always dreaded, and she knew if she looked at him exactly what expression would be in his eyes.

"And what are you suggesting by that?" she asked.

She spoke scathingly, hoping she would embarrass him by such a frank question.

"I am suggesting, Tatika," Lord Crowley replied, "that you should marry me."

For a moment Tatika felt that she could not have

heard him right. The next second she thought he was joking.

She turned to look at him. He was staring at her in a manner she most disliked, but there seemed, although she could hardly credit it, no doubt of his sincerity.

"If you are serious," she said, finding her voice with difficulty, "then I must thank Your Lordship for your offer and tell you that my answer is—no."

"Why not?"

Tatika was looking away from him across the garden.

"Is there any point in my answering that question?"

"Every point," he replied. "I want to know why you will not marry me. I have a great deal to offer you, Tatika."

"They are not the sort of things I want," Tatika answered.

"Then what do you want?" he enquired.

"I suppose the answer is—to fall in love," Tatika said.

"I will teach you to love me."

She shook her head.

"You know that is not possible. My father did not have to teach my mother, it was something that happened between them."

"Something which happens perhaps to two people in a million, that they should love each other simultaneously and immediately the first moment they meet," Lord Crowley said. "But I am a very experienced lover, Tatika, and I can teach you the delights of love far better than any feckless youth. You will learn to love me in time, and until then I shall enjoy arousing that wild Russian emotion I sense within you."

"I am sorry, My Lord, what you suggest is impossible."

"Nothing is impossible!" Lord Crowley said. "I

want you, Tatika, I wanted you from the very first moment I saw you."

"I think, My Lord, you will find it was but a passing fancy."

"That is where you are wrong," Lord Crowley said, "and I will show you how ignorant you are about me and about love."

He put out his hand as he spoke and took hers. She would have moved away from him, but he held it fast.

She was wearing gloves and she was thankful that she could not feel his bare hand, because even at his touch she felt herself recoil and knew that she found his proximity repulsive.

He would have put his other arm round her but she rose to her feet.

"There is nothing more to say, My Lord," she said quickly.

"I have a great deal more to say," he retorted, "but perhaps this is not the right place to say it. When can we meet?"

"I told you last night and I must tell you again," Tatika said, "that I do not wish to meet you, My Lord. We have nothing in common, nothing to discuss, nothing even to argue about."

He was still holding her hand so that she could not escape. Now he rose slowly to his feet still holding her captive.

"I see, Tatika," he said, "you are a very formidable adversary, but I am used to getting what I want in life! I want you and because I want you I intend to have you."

"You are making a mistake, My Lord," Tatika said. "I am not to be bought, coerced or bullied. I am deeply honoured that you should wish me to be your wife, but the answer is no, now and forever."

Lord Crowley gave a little laugh which she knew was characteristic of him.

"I find," he said, "it strangely exciting to be defied by something so small, so exquisite and so desirable. But let me assure you, Tatika, I am an indomitable fighter."

With a little effort, Tatika took her hand from his.

"I do not wish to fight you, My Lord," she answered in her coldest voice, "I just do not intend to see you again. Please do not waste your time by sending me flowers or invitations, they are neither of them acceptable."

"So aggressive," he exclaimed. "But as I said to you last night, I still want to kiss you."

"As I do not wish to appear conspicuous by leaving you and walking back to the house alone," Tatika said, "will you kindly escort me?"

"I will do that," Lord Crowley said, "and perhaps because I am obeying you it will count as a small mark in my favour."

They moved in silence until they reached the stone steps which led into the Ball-room. Couples were slowly coming in from the garden for the beginning of a new dance. Tatika looked up at Lord Crowley.

"Good night, My Lord," she said, "and goodbye."

"On the contrary, it is *au revoir*, Tatika. I promise you that we shall meet again and very shortly."

Tatika curtseyed and then without looking at him again walked up the steps to the Ball-room.

She found her Step-mother sitting on the dais with a number of other chaperons.

"Where have you been, Tatika?" she asked crossly. "And where is your partner?"

"He has gone home," Tatika answered. "I shall not see him again."

As she spoke she hoped it was the truth. She had an uncomfortable feeling she was being menaced.

There was something overpowering about Lord Crowley, something in his self-confidence, his conceit and unshakable assurance which made her afraid.

"I have shown him quite clearly that I dislike

him," she told herself. "He cannot in these circumstances wish to pursue me."

Yet she was uneasy because she knew she was afraid of him.

Chapter Three

"I am afraid we are late, Ellen," Tatika exclaimed.

"There is plenty of time, Miss Tatika," Ellen replied consolingly.

It was always the same: when Tatika became immersed in a book she forgot time and place and everything she had to do.

She was driving back with Ellen in a hackney carriage from the British Museum. She had spent the afternoon there and every second had been one of sheer enjoyment.

Ellen had been quite content to sit quietly and, as she put it herself, "to rest her legs."

She dozed a little from time to time and there was no-one to notice; in fact the Reading Room was almost empty.

"What are you so interested in now?" Ellen asked as the carriage moved slowly through the quiet squares towards Mayfair.

"To tell you the truth," Tatika smiled, "I am learning about England. Do you realise, Ellen, that we have lived so much abroad, that I really know very little about my own country?"

"It's not surprising," Ellen replied.

"I was ashamed of knowing so little about Austria when I arrived in Vienna, so by the time we left I really knew a great deal of its history," Tatika went on. "And although I was younger when Papa was in Rome, I did learn to speak Italian. I even tried to memorise the endless sequence of Popes! But now it is time to discover England."

She laughed as she spoke and said:

"I am starting almost at the beginning. Today I have been reading about the Vikings and how they conquered so much of the country. They must have been a magnificent race."

Ellen murmured something which Tatika knew was sympathetic.

Both she and Tatika were aware that she was just "someone to talk to" and was not expected to contribute to this sort of conversation.

"Can you imagine how strong, imaginative and brave they were?" Tatika went on. "Their armies sailed in small boats across the North Sea to conquer Northumbria and East Anglia and fight endless battles with the Earls of Orkney. They even went as far as the Hebrides and Ireland!"

She gave a little sigh.

"How I would like to have seen the Viking Chiefs with their horned helmets, carrying their shields and long-handled battle axes and wearing swords inlaid with gold and silver. They must have looked so handsome and exciting!"

"I expect they left a lot of misery behind them," Ellen remarked. "Wars have never done anyone any good!"

"That is true," Tatika agreed, "but at the same time I find it thrilling to read about the Vikings. If we can escape from Her Ladyship I must go back tomorrow, there is so much I want to learn."

"You'll be lucky if she doesn't wish to take you to a tea-party or make a round of calls," Ellen replied tartly.

She could never speak of Lady Lynch without her voice sharpening.

She had adored Tatika's mother and she was

willing to do anything for Sir Dominic. But she had
been up against Lady Lynch, whom she called scorn-
fully the "New Mistress," ever since she had become
Tatika's Step-mother.

Lady Lynch would undoubtedly have got rid of
the old maid, who she said often enough was not
"worth her keep," but she knew that such drastic action would be opposed not only by Tatika, but also
by Sir Dominic. ·

Ties with his first wife were still very strong.

Jealous and dictatorial though she might be, Lady
Lynch was shrewd enough to know that she must
tread carefully when it came to disparaging anything
which had been treasured by her predecessor.

No second wife likes to feel that the ghost of the
first still hovers in the background of her marriage.

A strong reason for Lady Lynch's dislike of Tatika was that she felt that every time Sir Dominic
looked at his daughter she reminded him of his dead
wife.

As they drove on Ellen also was thinking how
closely Tatika resembled her mother. The small
straight aristocratic nose, the soft curves of her lips,
the perfect oval of her face, her huge dark eyes were
completely Russian.

There was no reflection in her of her father's
handsome looks, and indeed Tatika's small bones and
lissom grace made it hard to believe that she was in
fact half-English.

The hackney carriage drew up outside 26 Charles
Street. Tatika jumped out before the cabman could
get down from the box and opened her reticule to
pay him.

He took off his tall hat as he accepted the money,
and she thanked him with a sweet smile before, followed by Ellen, she entered the house.

"I will go straight upstairs," Tatika said in a low
voice.

But as she took a step towards the staircase, the
Butler came from the other side of the hall to say:

"The Master and Her Ladyship are in the Drawing-room, Miss Tatika. They have asked to see you immediately on your return."

"They are waiting for me now?" Tatika asked.

"Yes, Miss."

Tatika gave a quick glance at the grandfather-clock. This would mean she would be late for dinner and she knew how disagreeable that would make her Step-mother.

But there was nothing that she could do but obey the summons. She ran quickly up the stairs and opened the door of the Drawing-room expecting to find her father and Step-mother already changed into evening-dress.

Instead she saw at a quick glance that they were still in their afternoon clothes and were standing in front of the mantelpiece talking earnestly.

As she entered the room Lady Lynch gave a cry.

"Tatika, we have been waiting for you! Where could you have been?"

"Waiting for me?" Tatika enquired.

"Yes, dear, to tell you how thrilled we are, how delighted! Really you were a very clever girl! Why did you not tell me last night?"

Tatika looked at her Step-mother in bewilderment. She had never known her so pleasant, and then her eyes went to her father.

Sir Dominic was also smiling and he held out his hand.

"My dearest," he said pulling her close to him, "I cannot tell you how happy this has made me."

"I am sorry, Papa," Tatika said, "but I do not know what you are talking about."

"Now really, Tatika, you cannot expect us to believe that," Lady Lynch interposed before Sir Dominic could speak. "Lord Crowley has only just left and he has made us both the happiest people in the world."

Tatika was very still.

"Lord Crowley?" she asked, and as she spoke his

name she felt as if a cold hand had been laid on her heart.

Her father's arm tightened round her shoulders.

"Crowley has asked me formally for your hand in marriage, my dear," he said, "although I understand he has already spoken of it to you."

Tatika drew in a deep breath and disengaged herself from her father's embrace.

"Lord Crowley asked me last night to marry him," she said quietly, "and I refused him."

"You what?"

Lady Lynch's question was almost a scream.

"I told him quite firmly," Tatika said, "that I will not marry him and that I did not wish to see him again."

"Are you insane?"

Lady Lynch appeared to have difficulty in speaking.

"What are you saying, Tatika?" her father asked. "I understood from Crowley that you had discussed the question of marriage."

"He asked me to be his wife," Tatika said, "and I find such an idea is impossible."

"Do you know what you are saying?" Lady Lynch asked furiously. "Do you realise that Lord Crowley is one of the richest men in England? He has everything! Houses, possessions, wealth, a position at Court! When you marry him, Tatika, you will be one of the Marlborough House Set."

The words seemed to spill out of Lady Lynch's mouth, but Tatika only looked at her father.

"I cannot marry him, Papa," she said firmly.

"Now listen, Tatika," Sir Dominic said uneasily, avoiding his daughter's eyes. "I realise that Crowley is older than you, but he has tremendous assets. He can give you all the things I would wish you to have and he is obviously completely infatuated."

"He loves you," Lady Lynch cried. "He loves you enough to marry you! Surely that is enough? Can you really consider turning down a suitor whom any other girl in England would give her eyes to marry?"

Tatika did not answer. She was still watching her father.

"It is like this, Tatika," Sir Dominic said slowly. "Crowley is, I admit, much older than you, but would you be happy with a young man? You are clever, you have always been too clever for your years and far more intelligent than any of your contemporaries."

He paused before he continued:

"You have also lived a somewhat unusual life. I cannot help feeling that an older man would appreciate your many talents and would be more likely to make you happy."

"That is diplomatic talk, Papa, and you know it," Tatika retorted. "Lord Crowley may be able to give me many material things which I lack at the moment, but I do not love him and I will not marry anyone I do not love."

"Do not listen to her, Dominic!" Lady Lynch exclaimed furiously. "What does a child of eighteen know about love or marriage? It is the best offer that Tatika is likely to have in the whole of her life. You would be doing her a disservice if you allow her through some childish, romantic idiocy to turn down such a suitor."

Sir Dominic looked at the clock on the mantelpiece.

"You are putting me in a very difficult position, Tatika," he said. "I have, as it happens, given my consent to your marriage and I have promised we will all dine at Crowley House."

"Then I am afraid Papa, that you must go without me," Tatika said. "I do not wish to marry Lord Crowley and therefore I cannot dine with him tonight. Please make my apologies."

She turned and walked from the room with a composure that she was far from feeling.

Only when she had shut the door of the

Drawing-room behind her did she pick up her skirts and run up the next flight of stairs to her bed-room.

She burst into the room and stood for a moment with her back against the door, her hands crossed on her breast as if to quell the tumult within her.

"Lord Crowley has been clever," she thought, "very clever."

He had out-manoeuvred her once again by approaching her father.

He would have known that her Step-mother would be overjoyed at the thought of such a marriage, and it was not difficult to see that her father was also bemused by the glittering picture of wealth and consequence which was being dangled in front of his eyes.

Tatika drew a deep breath, then putting her hands up to her face walked across the room to sit down on the stool in front of the dressing-table.

This was something she had not expected, and she told herself that she was going to have to fight hard not to be pressured into marrying a man she knew she not only distrusted but actively loathed.

"I hate him," she told herself, "there is something about him which frightens me."

She knew too that he was a dangerous adversary. She was quite certain he would stop at nothing to get his own way and his first move had been, she had to admit to herself, a clever one.

She heard the door open behind her and thought it was Ellen coming to lay out her clothes for dinner.

Then she saw reflected in the mirror on the dressing-table not Ellen but her Step-mother.

Lady Lynch came into the room and closed the door behind her.

"I want to talk to you, Tatika."

Tatika rose from the stool and stood facing her Step-mother.

"There is nothing to discuss," she said. "I am sorry if I have disappointed you and Papa, but I cannot and will not marry Lord Crowley."

Lady Lynch walked towards her.

"Can you really be so selfish," she asked, "so ungrateful, so utterly indifferent to your father whom you have always professed to love?"

"Papa would not have worried about my marrying someone if you had not kept harping on the subject," Tatika replied. "He is fond of me and I know that he likes having me in his house, whatever you may say to the contrary."

"He may like having you but he cannot afford you," Lady Lynch said acidly. "Can you not get that into your head? He cannot afford to keep a daughter."

"He managed to do so before he married."

"That was different," Lady Lynch snapped. "You know as well as I do that his private income is not a large one, and at the moment he is in debt—deeply in debt."

Tatika was about to reply that if that was the truth it was Lady Lynch's fault and caused entirely by her extravagance. Then she realised there was no point in arguing.

Instead she said quietly:

"I will marry when I meet someone whom I can love. Until then, I am afraid you will just have to put up with me."

"And you really intend to refuse Lord Crowley?"

"I have already told you so."

"Can you not understand what it will mean, not only to you but to us?" Lady Lynch asked. "Lord Crowley is a close friend of the Prince of Wales. Through you we will be invited to all the great houses of England—houses whose doors are not open at the moment to your father."

She drew in her breath.

"You will be asked to stay with the Duke and Duchess of Portland at Welbeck, with the Devonshires at Chatsworth, with the Beauforts at Badminton. You will meet all the fascinating and exciting people who surround the Prince. Does that mean nothing to you?"

"Very little, I am afraid," Tatika answered. "I do not suppose that the people you mention are very different from those I have already met either with Papa or at the endless succession of social parties I have attended these last two months. After all one does not marry just to meet people."

"That is not true!" Lady Lynch contradicted. "Everyone who is normal wishes to meet the best of society, to move in Royal Circles, to be someone of consequence. And that is exactly what you will be as the wife of one of the most important men in England."

"A man who is at least twenty-five years older than I am," Tatika answered.

"What does that matter, you stupid little fool?" Lady Lynch asked furiously.

"I am sorry, Step-mama," Tatika said in a tired voice, "but I will not be bullied into marrying this man. I dislike him—do you understand?—I dislike him and I will not be his wife whatever you may say."

She faced her Step-mother defiantly. Losing her temper Lady Lynch reached out her hand and smacked Tatika hard across the cheek.

Tatika was so much smaller and more frail than the older woman, that she staggered.

Then, keeping her balance, she put her hand up to her cheek to stand staring at her Step-mother's face contorted with fury.

"You will marry him," Lady Lynch said through gritted teeth, "you will marry him, because if you do not appreciate the position he can give you, I do. I want to be *persona grata* with the people you dismiss so airily. It would mean a great deal to your father, and I will not allow you to throw away what is the most splendid chance that any girl has ever been offered!"

Lady Lynch almost spat the words at her and then she said:

"You may think that you can defy me, but you will find it difficult to do so. You will dine with Lord Crowley tonight and you will agree to marry him if I have to beat you insensible."

"Are you really threatening me physically?" Tatika asked.

"Make no mistake about it!" Lady Lynch said slowly. "I will beat you until you agree to what I ask, if I have to get the servants to hold you down while I do so."

There was so much venom in her voice that Tatika instinctively took a step backwards, her hands still on her burning cheek.

Lady Lynch noticed it and said with an unpleasant smile:

"You will find that I mean what I am saying. You have been lamentably spoiled all your life, because your father is weak. He has always been weak where women are concerned. But I am strong and tough, Tatika, as you will find out!"

Her voice sharpened as she went on .

"Your screams will not worry me, and when you have screamed yourself into unconsciousness you will do what I ask, or I will continue to beat you day after day until you can no longer speak."

It was impossible not to believe that Lady Lynch meant what she said.

There was something horrible in the manner in which she spoke, in the narrowing of her eyes, in the sharp lines etching her face through the violence of her feelings.

The two women looked at each other and for a moment Tatika thought her Step-mother was going to strike her again.

She braced herself for the blow. Then shaking with anger Lady Lynch walked to the mantelpiece and put up her hand towards the bell-pull.

"Which is it to be?" she asked harshly. "Do you agree to come out to dinner tonight, or do I call for two of the housemaids to hold you down while I beat you?"

"You really believe they ... would do that?" Tatika asked.

She could not credit this was happening to her, and yet there was no misunderstanding the ugliness of Lady Lynch's expression and the positive manner in which she spoke.

"They will do it," Lady Lynch replied, "because if they do not obey me they leave this house tonight without a reference. What servant is going to risk that? So tell me, Tatika, do I ring this bell, or do you accompany us to dinner at Crowley House?"

There was a look in her Step-mother's eyes which told Tatika all too clearly that she would actually enjoy beating her.

She had always known that Lady Lynch disliked her, but she had not realised how violent her animosity was, or that beneath the pleasantly suave facade she presented to the world, there lay the coarse vulgarity of a fish-wife.

"Which is it to be?" Lady Lynch insisted, her fingers tightening on the bell-rope.

Tatika made up her mind.

"I will dine at Crowley House."

Lady Lynch dropped her arm.

"I thought you would see sense!" she said. "But remember, Tatika, you will also be pleasant to Lord Crowley. If he cries off because of anything you have said, then I swear I will half-murder you and I am not speaking lightly."

She walked towards the door.

"You have twenty-five minutes in which to change," she said, "and do not be late. I have learned how to handle you now, my girl, and it is a lesson I shall not forget in the future."

She went out of the room and slammed the door behind her. Tatika sank down on a chair and put her hands over her eyes.

This could not be true, this could not be happen-

ing to her! How was it possible that her Step-mother
could behave in such a manner or that she could find
herself caught in a trap from which for the moment
she could not see a way of escape?

The door opened and Ellen came in. Tatika rose
and ran towards her.

"Oh, Ellen! Ellen!" she cried. "What am I to do?"

"I heard what was being said!" Ellen replied.
"How that wicked woman dares to speak to you like
that I've no idea! I cannot believe the Master would
put up with it if he knew."

"What is the point of telling him?" Tatika asked.
"He also wishes me to marry Lord Crowley."

"Do you dislike the gentleman so much?" Ellen
asked.

"I loathe him!" Tatika replied. "And all this is his
fault! I will never forgive him for it."

Ellen looked at the clock.

"But you have promised to dine with His Lordship, Miss Tatika, and there is no point in putting the
new Mistress in a worse rage than she is in at the moment."

Tatika gave a deep sigh and stood quietly as Ellen
undressed her as if she were a child.

There was no time for a bath, but she washed
herself and put on one of the elegant and very becoming gowns that Lady Lynch had helped her
choose at the beginning of the Season.

Unpleasant though she might be, Lady Lynch
had excellent taste and Tatika had chosen her own
clothes ever since her mother's death.

Between the two of them the gowns in which
Tatika graced the Season had been a perfect frame
for her dark beauty.

While some of her dresses were white, as was
conventional for a débutante, others because they became her better were in clear colours which seemed
to accentuate the darkness of her hair, the perfection
of her skin and the grace of her movements.

Deep in her thoughts, Tatika had no idea what

she was wearing until Ellen fetched a velvet wrap of deep emerald green from the wardrobe and put it round her shoulders.

She then saw that she was dressed in a gown of green silk trimmed with frill upon frill of tulle which made her look as if she were a sprite from the woodlands or a nymph rising from the green depths of the sea.

She wore no jewelry, for she needed none. The rounded perfection of her neck and the tips of her shoulders were vividly white against the transparent tulle which softened the low déolletage of her bodice.

Tulle frills flowed out behind her from the bustle at the back of her gown and she heard the gentle "fru-fru" as she went down the stairs where her father and Step-mother were waiting.

Sir Dominic looked at his watch to show without saying anything that she was late, but Lady Lynch merely looked at Tatika with a cruel expression in her eyes.

"She is enjoying her power over me," Tatika thought and holding her head very high she followed her Step-mother into the carriage which was waiting outside for them.

They drove in silence. Tatika had the feeling that her father wished to say something consiliatory but was afraid of his wife.

Lady Lynch was, she knew, gloating over the fact that she was for the moment threatened into submission.

Knowing her Step-mother's mind, Tatika was well aware that the threat of being beaten, if not the actual performance, would be held over her and reiterated day after day until finally in desperation she would be glad to escape from her home.

But that could only be possible at the expense of surrendering herself to a man she detested!

"There must be something I can do," she thought, but knew that for the moment she was too agitated to think clearly.

Something told her she must play for time.

It was no use exhausting her energies in fighting a battle she could not quickly win. She must conserve her strength for her main objective, which was not to marry Lord Crowley.

The carriage came to a standstill and Lady Lynch was unable to refrain from remarking spitefully as Sir Dominic alighted:

"Do not forget what I said to you, Tatika! If you say anything to make him 'cry off,' you will suffer in a manner which at the moment is beyond your imagination."

Tatika did not reply and Lady Lynch with a rustle of silk, her diamonds glinting, swept through the porticoed door of Crowley House.

Their host was waiting for them in a Salon which Tatika realised exceeded the magnificence of any private house she had ever visited.

She had enough knowledge of art to realise that the Van Dykes on the walls were superlative, that there was a masterpiece by Turner, Gainsborough, and Reynolds everywhere she looked.

The furniture was equalled only by pieces she had admired at Buckingham Palace or in the British Embassies abroad.

But it was difficult to be conscious of anything save the over-powering presence of Lord Crowley.

He seemed bigger, more awe-inspiring and even more self-assured against the background of his own possessions than he had appeared on the two previous occasions that she had met him.

He greeted Lady Lynch first, then turned to Tatika. She curtsied and kept her eyes downcast.

"I want to welcome you to my house, Tatika," he said.

She hated the note in his voice which told her that he was triumphant because as he well knew, she had been brought there against her will.

He shook hands with Sir Dominic and while the

three older people sipped a glass of sherry, Tatika looked around her.

"All this could be mine," she thought and knew that none of it was of any interest because included with it went the owner.

The dinner-table was decorated with the same kind of orchids that Lord Crowley had sent her the previous day. She knew he intended her to remember that he had said they reminded him of her.

Tatika deliberately made herself appear dull and stupid.

She answered any questions put to her if possible in a monosyllable and occupied herself by pretending to eat the excellent food that was offered her.

She hoped that Lord Crowley would realise what a very poor bargain he was getting in a girl who was so obtuse and so obviously unintelligent.

But once she met his eyes and realised he saw through her pretence and was merely amused by her play-acting.

Dinner seemed to take a long time although Tatika realised that in reality it occupied no more than the hour that the Prince of Wales insisted was long enough for a meal, however many courses were served.

Then Lady Lynch and Tatika left the gentlemen to their port and went up the carved staircase to the bed-rooms on the second floor.

The rooms were magnificent. Huge beds covered in priceless antique lace, carved gold carollas from which flowed curtains of taffeta, silk and gauze.

The dressing-table mirrors were framed with carved wood, gilded and ornamented with coronets, and the pictures were as good as those Tatika had noticed downstairs.

There were two maids to attend to them, to pull out the flounces on their dresses and to bring them anything they required.

There was no chance of Lady Lynch speaking to Tatika privately until they went down to the Salon, to find the gentlemen had not yet left the Dining-room.

It was then Lady Lynch said with a note of greed in her voice:

"Have you ever seen a more fabulous house? If this does not make you more interested in this marriage, nothing will."

Tatika did not answer. She had no intention at this moment of entering into an argument with her Step-mother, in which she knew she could easily come off worse.

"You are lucky, more lucky than you deserve to be," Lady Lynch said enviously, "and I hope when you are hostess here that you will not forget all that your father has done for you these last eighteen years, and that owning so much will not give you a swollen head."

Tatika walked across the room to look at a table on which there was arranged a number of valuable snuff-boxes.

Mostly of enamel, set in gold and ornamented with diamonds, there were many of great historical interest. As she picked up one to examine it more closely, Lady Lynch said bitterly:

"God! If I had only had your chances, what I would have made of my life!"

Tatika put down the snuff-box which she read inside had been given to "Charles James Fox by his affectionate friend, George, Prince of Wales."

She was trying to think of the gay Georgian days and the Bucks and Fops who had carried such snuff-boxes, rather than of the predicament in which she found herself at this present moment, when the door opened and the men came in.

At the sight of Lord Crowley and the sound of his voice, she felt a sudden tremor run through her and knew it was fear.

For one moment she felt panic-stricken. She was caught, captured and soon she would be imprisoned for life and there would be no escape!

Then with the self-control she had exercised for so long in her life, she walked calmly and quietly to her father's side.

As if he half sensed what she was feeling, Sir Dominic took her hand in his. He felt the coldness of her fingers and the manner in which they trembled.

"We have been talking about horses," he said conversationally.

Tatika knew that he was trying to dispel her fears and make her feel there was nothing unusual or disturbing about the evening.

"There is something I want to show you in the next room, Lady Lynch," Lord Crowley said.

"More treasures?" Lady Lynch asked archly. "There are so many of them."

"I shall look forward to your inspecting my other possessions," Lord Crowley replied. "I have some very fine pictures at Crowley Park. The Prince and Princess of Wales will be staying with me for Goodwood and I do hope I can persuade you all to come as my guests."

If Tatika had not been so frightened, she would have been amused at the rapturous expression on her Step-mother's face. Then as Lady Lynch moved beside Lord Crowley into the other room, she turned to her father.

"What am I to do, Papa?" she asked almost in a whisper.

He made no pretence of not understanding what she meant.

"I am sure your Step-mother is right," he said uneasily.

"I cannot do it, Papa."

"You will have to," he answered. "There is no alternative."

He was taking the line of least resistance as he always did where his wife was concerned, and Tatika knew she would have little help from him. Sir Dominic hated scenes. He liked women to be soft, complaisant, accommodating and very feminine.

He would never assert himself, Tatika was sure, to the point of opposing his wife when Lady Lynch was as determined as she was now.

She gave a little sigh. She knew she would have to rely entirely on herself.

Lord Crowley came back into the room alone.

"Your wife asks you to join her," he said to Sir Dominic.

He was manoeuvering, Tatika knew, so that he could be alone with her. She wanted to protest, but what could she say? As Sir Dominic obediently went through the door into the other room, she faced Lord Crowley proudly, her eyes on his.

"I have been clever, little Tatika," he said disarmingly.

"Very clever," Tatika agreed.

"What have you done to your cheek?"

Tatika put her fingers against the place where her Step-mother had hit her. It was still burning and she realised now it must be a crimson mark against the whiteness of her skin.

"Need you ask?"

"Do you mean your Step-mother hit you?"

"She not only hit me," Tatika answered, "but she threatened that if I did not dine here tonight and agree to marry you, she would beat me insensible while the servants held me down."

She spoke bitterly, hoping to shame him into an expression of embarrassment or at least of surprise. Instead, even as she spoke, she realised she had made a mistake.

She saw a glant of something repulsive and terrifying in his eyes as he said with a smile:

"I thought I should have help from that quarter."

"I had hoped you would at least fight me singlehanded," Tatika said quickly.

"I have told you that I always get what I want," he replied, "and all is fair in love and war! There are no Queensbury Rules for me, Tatika."

"So I perceive," she said scathingly.

"Surely to escape such violence you will be willing to marry me rather sooner than I first anticipated?" he asked.

"Can you really want me under such circumstances?" Tatika enquired. "What pleasure could there be in having a wife who is dragged almost senseless to the altar, beaten into submission and forced by sheer physical exhaustion to accede to your desires?"

Lord Crowley threw back his head and laughed.

"You entrance me!" he exclaimed. "You are not only beautiful, you are intelligent, you have courage and you are a fighter. I like fighting, Tatika, when I know that I shall be the victor."

She turned her head away because she did not want him to see that she was afraid. Then he said in a different tone:

"At the same time I would not wish you to be unhappy tonight. Let me give you a present that will please you."

He took something as he spoke from his pocket and taking her left hand in his he put a ring on her finger.

For a moment Tatika could think only how she disliked his touching her.

Then she saw the ring was an enormous emerald, so large it made her hand look very small and frail and yet inevitably enhanced the beauty of it.

Surrounded by diamonds, the emerald seemed not only to glitter but to have strange depths in it.

"It is a family ring," Lord Crowley explained, "and there is a tiara, necklace, bracelets and other pieces to match. Emeralds become you, Tatika, as no other stones could do."

Tatika did not answer. She was thinking that the emerald, beautiful though it might be, was like a chain binding her to this man whose very proximity made her shiver with a strange fear.

"And now will you thank me?" Lord Crowley asked.

Intent on her thoughts she did not realise what he intended until his arms went round her.

She made a convulsive movement to escape, but it was too late. He pulled her roughly against him and holding her so tightly that she could not move he put his hand under her little chin and lifted her face to his.

For a moment he looked down at her and she saw an expression in his eyes which frightened her as she had never been frightened before.

This was not an ordinary man of the type she had managed so far to avoid so adroitly! He was sinister, evil and he made her feel trapped and helpless.

"There is no escape, Tatika!" Lord Crowley said as if he could read her thoughts.

Then even as she struggled ineffectively against him, his mouth was on hers.

His lips were hard, brutal and greedy. Tatika had never been kissed before, but she knew there was something bestial in the manner in which his mouth took possession of hers.

It was not love which Lord Crowley felt for her but lust, and with it a cruelty that she sensed rather than understood.

He desired her in a manner which even in her innocence Tatika was aware was lewd and perverted. It was not what a decent man should feel for the woman he thought of as his wife.

With a superhuman effort, she clamped her own lips together and held herself rigid.

Her whole body became stiff and she concentrated every nerve on resisting him rather than struggle fruitlessly against his superior strength.

For a moment he was too obsessed by his own desire to realise what she was doing. Then he raised his head and looked down at her.

"So you hate me as much as that!" he exclaimed. "But I promise you, Tatika, I will break you and conquer you in the end, and I shall enjoy doing so more than I have ever enjoyed anything in my whole life."

Chapter Four

Tatika slept very little during that night and when she did she awoke with a feeling of horror that she was being pursued and could not run fast enough to get away.

When Ellen came in at eight o'clock with her early-morning tea she sat up in bed and said:

"Ellen, I am desperate! I know Mama would not have wished me to marry Lord Crowley, but how can I avoid it?"

Ellen put down a tray containing a pot of tea, a cup, a small jug of milk, and a very thin slice of bread and butter. Then she crossed the room and drew back the curtains.

"I've been thinking about you all night, Miss Tatika," she said in a worried tone, "and I can't see that there's anything you can do."

"I will not marry him! It is impossible!"

"Why do you feel so strongly about this particular gentleman?" Ellen asked.

"I do not quite know the answer to that," Tatika replied. "But there is something about him which I know is wicked and evil. It is something which really frightens me and you know I am never wrong in my judgment of people."

"That's true, Miss Tatika," Ellen agreed, "and

58

your mother was just the same. Sometimes she would say to me, 'Ellen, that man is bad!' and she was always proved to be right."

"Well, I know Lord Crowley is bad," Tatika said, "so I will not marry him. It is utterly and completely impossible for me to do so; I would rather die.

"Don't talk like that," Ellen said sharply.

"I mean it," Tatika insisted. "I would rather take my own life than be married to such a man."

"Even to say such a thing is a sin against God," Ellen remarked almost crossly.

"Then help me!" Tatika cried. "Help me to find a way of escape!"

Ellen made a helpless gesture and her kind face was deeply perturbed as she looked at Tatika sitting up in bed, her dark hair falling over her shoulders.

Her eyes were dark with misery, her expression despondent. It was when she was in despair that she looked most Russian, most like her mother.

"You must not be unhappy, my dearie!" Ellen exclaimed. "I vowed when your mother first put you in my arms, after you were born, that I would look after you. And you know that since she died I have felt as if you were my own child."

"What can I do?"

"The New Mistress is determined you should marry this gentleman, and who can oppose her?"

"I could run away," Tatika suggested.

"And what would you live on?" Ellen asked.

"I would have to get work of some sort," Tatika said vaguely.

"What work is there for a Lady like yourself?" Ellen asked. "Even for Parson's daughters the only available employment is that of being a governess or a companion."

Tatika raised her head and looked at Ellen with a sudden light in her eyes.

"Companion!" she cried. "That is a job I could do quite easily. Do you remember Miss Greaves who was with Grand-mama? She was a timid, rather frightened old maid, but we were all fond of her. I had a letter from her at Easter saying she had reached Australia and was very happy to be with her brother and his wife."

"Miss Greaves was over forty," Ellen said.

"Surely old people would be happy to have someone young to look after them and to do all the things Miss Greaves did. After all they were not very difficult."

Tatika started to count on her fingers.

"Miss Greaves used to read to Grand-mama. She would change her library books. She would do the flowers. She arranged the places for dinner and wrote letters when Grand-mama was too ill or too lazy to write them herself."

Tatika threw out her hands.

"I could do all those things. And what is more, I am sure I would have plenty of time to read, or to translate books if I could get a publisher to trust me with one."

"It is impossible!" Ellen said abruptly. "You are a Lady, Miss Tatika. It is not for someone like you to go waiting on another Lady however distinguished she might be."

"I will scrub floors, I will work in a scullery, I will do anything rather than marry Lord Crowley," Tatika cried passionately.

She got out of bed.

"Ellen, I have an idea! This morning I am going to the Domestic Agency in Mount Street to see if they have a suitable position for me on their books."

"It is a crazy idea! I will not let you do it," Ellen exclaimed hotly.

Tatika smiled at her.

"And how are you going to stop me?" she asked. "Speak to my Step-mother? You would never do that to me, Ellen."

"I beg you, Miss Tatika, do not do anything so

wild, so foolish," Ellen said. "Heaven knows what trouble you might find yourself in."

"I might find myself in more trouble if I become a governess," Tatika said slowly. "I have heard stories of how young governesses are pursued by the Master of the house or an older son.

"It may be true or it may be untrue, but I do not wish to put myself in the position where I encounter men. I am sick of them—do you hear me, Ellen? I am sick of all men. I would be happy if I never saw a man again!"

"You're talking foolish as you well know, Miss Tatika," Ellen protested. "With your looks it would be a sin against nature to go shutting yourself away with a lot of women. Besides, wherever you go you'll encounter jealousy. There'll always be women like the New Mistress who'll feel spiteful because you're putting them in the shade."

"I will work for someone so old she will not worry about me," Tatika smiled.

The sadness had gone from her eyes, she no longer looked despondent. She felt that she could do something. She could at least explore this new avenue of escape and the idea gave her hope.

"What is my Step-mother doing this morning?" she asked.

"I heard Her Ladyship has ordered the carriage for 9:30 because she has an appointment at the dentist," Ellen replied.

"Then that is our opportunity," Tatika said. "I will dress now, Ellen, and go down to breakfast quite normally. As soon as Her Ladyship has left, you and I will set off for Mount Street."

She paused a moment. Then she said:

"You remember that black dress I wore last year when I was in mourning for Grand-mama, the one you disliked because you said it was unbecoming and too old for me? I am sure you have it upstairs somewhere."

"Yes, I have it," Ellen said briefly.

"Then please bring it here and put it in the wardrobe," Tatika said, "and bring the little black bonnet I used to wear with it. Another thing, Ellen, I will borrow your sewing-glasses, they will make me look older."

"Miss Tatika, you can't be serious about this!" Ellen cried. "It's a nonsensical idea, as you well know. No-one would take you as companion looking as you do—besides you have no references."

"I have already thought of that," Tatika replied. "I noticed two or three days ago, Ellen, that downstairs in the drawer where Her Ladyship keeps her writing-paper engraved with this address, there are also some sheets of paper headed The Manor House, St. Albans."

"They must have come from your Grandmother's after she died," Ellen exclaimed.

"Of course they did," Tatika replied, "and I am going to use them to write myself a reference."

"You can't do that, Miss Tatika!" Ellen exclaimed in horror. "It's forgery."

"It will not be, because I shall write it in my own name," Tatika answered. "I shall write exactly the recommendation I should have given Miss Greaves, or Papa would have done, if she had asked for one before she went to Australia. The only reason she did not want a reference was that she was retiring."

"No good will come of this!" Ellen said positively.

"If it saves me from marrying Lord Crowley it be the greatest good possible! I intend to disappear!" Tatika said.

Then after a short pause she added slowly:

"Even if I eventually have to come home, it will make Papa realise that I am serious in refusing to marry His Lordship. Perhaps when he misses me he will be sorry that he gave in to my Step-mother."

"Oh, my dearie, don't do anything so foolish," Ellen begged. "You may run into far worse trouble than having to marry a Gentleman like His Lordship."

"It could not be worse! Nothing whatever could be worse!" Tatika declared passionately.

Then she said with almost a happy look on her face:

"Come on, Ellen, we cannot be faint-hearted, you and I. There is so much to do!"

The Domestic Bureau on Mount Street was, as Tatika knew, one of the most reputable places in London for the engagement of Gentleman's servants.

She had never herself entered the place, because after Sir Dominic's second marriage her Step-mother would not allow her any share in management of staff.

But on several occasions Tatika had waited outside in the carriage while Lady Lynch had gone into the Bureau to interview a housemaid, or to replace kitchen staff who had found the bad temper of Sir Dominic's French chef intolerable.

But though she had not visited this particular Bureau, Tatika had a considerable experience in engaging servants for various houses and even his Embassies before her father remarried.

Men servants were of course always inspected by Sir Dominic's secretary, and then he interviewed them to make a final decision.

But where the womenfolk were concerned, he had been content to let Tatika choose the housemaids, kitchen and scullery maids, finding she was extremely proficient in picking girls who would be hard-working, respectable and not too greedy for high wages.

Tatika, as she entered Mrs. Bryant's Domestic Bureau, could not help feeling a flicker of amusement at the fact that now she was not in the role of employer, but of employee.

Dressed in the deep black which Ellen had rightly said was un-becoming, with her hair arranged unfashionably in a bun at the back of her head, and wearing Ellen's steel-rimmed spectacles, she looked a drab figure if one did not look too closely at her face.

It was however impossible to disguise the perfection of her features or hide the fact that she was actually very young.

"What is your name?" Mrs. Bryant's assistant, who sat at a desk with a large ledger in front of her, asked sharply.

"Miss Bray," Tatika answered.

"And your age?"

"Twenty-six."

The assistant looked at her with a slight expression of surprise, and Mrs. Bryant at the next desk, who had appeared not to be listening, remarked:

"You look younger than that!"

She was a middle-aged woman with iron-grey hair and a hard expression, due doubtless to dealing for many years with querulous employers and inefficient girls from the country, who expected to find situations where they were paid highly to do as little as possible.

"I am always told so," Tatika said complisantly. "I feel it will stand me in good stead in twenty years time."

"And what sort of employment are you seeking?" the assistant asked.

"Companion to an elderly lady," Tatika answered. "I have here a reference from the Granddaughter of the Honourable Mrs. Lynch which speaks very highly of my capabilities."

As she spoke she drew out the reference she had written herself on her Grand-mother's writing-paper.

To Whom It May Concern,

Miss Bray was in the employment of my Grand-mother, the Honourable Mrs. Harold Lynch until her death in April 1885. We were, as a family, all extremely fond of Miss Bray and deeply grateful for the kindness, consideration and affection she gave to my

Grand-mother during the three years she was in her employment and especially during the illness which terminated in her death.

I and my father, Sir Dominic Lynch, will be pleased to recommend Miss Bray at any time as we cannot speak too highly of her capabilities and her character.

Tatika Lynch.

The assistant read the letter and passed it to Mrs. Bryant. She read it through slowly, her face quite expressionless.

"This seems satisfactory," she said. "The difficulty is we have few positions for a companion on our books at the present moment. You would wish to be in London?"

"Oh no," Tatika said, "not in London. I would much prefer the country."

She thought that Mrs. Bryant seemed to think that was a point in her favour. The assistant turned the leaves of the large ledger and said in a whisper which was however quite audible to Tatika:

"There is really no-one except the Dowager Duchess of Strathcraig."

Mrs. Bryant turned to look at the ledger as if she thought she could see a name which had been omitted.

"She would not be suitable," the assistant said, still in a voice that Tatika could hear, "they particularly asked for someone middle-aged. Besides . . ."

"Would you object to Scotland?" Mrs. Bryant asked Tatika in a tone which seemed to indicate she already knew the answer.

"I would very much like to go to Scotland," Tatika replied.

She was trying to remember where she had heard the name Strathcraig before. Somehow it rang a bell in her mind.

Then she remembered her Step-mother and the

Ambassadress speaking of the Duke at the State Ball at Buckingham Palace.

"Castle Craig is very isolated," Mrs. Bryant said as if she was almost trying to put Tatika off, "and most of the companions we have sent there find it too lonely."

"The last one said it was sinister and gave her the creeps," the assistant contributed with a giggle.

"That is enough, Miss Lee," Mrs. Bryant said sharply. "Miss Robinson was an extremely nervous woman and not really the type I should ordinarily recommend."

The assistant pushed the book an inch or two away from her and said firmly:

"Well there's no other situation available at the moment."

"I would be prepared to go to Craig Castle," Tatika said quietly. "Is the position that of companion to the Duchess?"

"No indeed," the assistant answered before Mrs. Bryant could speak. "The Duchess is dead."

As she spoke Tatika remembered the Ambassadress saying something about "a tragedy," and then Mrs. Bryant interposed:

"It is the Dowager Duchess of Strathcraig, mother of the present Duke, who requires a companion. I will be frank with you, Miss Bray, and say that I do not think you are really suitable to fill the requirements that have been demanded. The gentleman who writes on behalf of the Dowager Duchess has asked particularly for someone middle-aged."

She paused before she added:

"I must also be truthful and tell you it is not an easy position. Two companions we have supplied have left the Castle this year and one last year."

"Because it was too isolated?" Tatika asked.

"That was the reason they gave us," Mrs. Bryant said with a meaningful glance at Miss Lee which checked any comment she might make.

"There is something strange here," Tatika

thought, but at the same time she felt that Scotland would be a perfect place to hide.

Who would think to look for her in Craig Castle? And surely as the companion of a Dowager Duchess she would not be exposed to the dangers and difficulties that Ellen anticipated she might encounter?

"How soon can I take up the position?" she asked.

"If you are prepared to apply for it," Mrs. Bryant said, "I must of course write to . . ."

She consulted the ledger.

". . . To Mr. Torquill McCraig who is the Controller of the household. The letter will take about four or five days to reach Scotland and the same amount of time for us to receive their reply."

"I am afraid I cannot wait as long as that," Tatika said firmly. "I require employment immediately."

There was a moment's silence. Then Miss Lee said nervously:

"We did send Miss Robinson and Miss Bell without waiting for an answer."

"The results were not very successful," Mrs. Bryant retorted.

Then looking at Tatika she said reluctantly:

"Very well, if you cannot wait, and because I have no-one else on my books at the moment with whom I could oblige a very valuable client, I will send a letter off today saying that you will leave London on Friday or Saturday."

"I will go on Friday, the day after tomorrow," Tatika said.

"The Dowager Duchess is extremely generous in providing the fare in advance and also paying the return fare to London of any companion who finds the position unsupportable," Mrs. Bryant said. "Your salary will be £50 a year and I am empowered to provide you with a second-class ticket to Glasgow."

She consulted the ledger before she continued.

"From Glasgow I understand you can either take the newly-opened Highland Railway which may involve a lot of changes, or you can travel by steamer on the Caledonian Canal to Inverness. Four pounds are allotted for travelling expenses from Glasgow onwards. When you reach Inverness you have, I believe, to take a horse-drawn carriage to carry you to the Castle."

As she finished speaking, Mrs. Bryant picked up the reference that was lying on the table and looked at it again.

"It certainly sounds as if you might suit Her Grace," she said, "but we have been disappointed before. I can only hope, Miss Bray, I am not making a mistake in sending someone so young to take what I consider a most responsible position."

"I shall do my best not to fail your trust in me," Tatika said humbly.

"If you will call here tomorrow, Thursday morning, I will have your ticket ready for you and a letter of introduction just in case the letter we shall send today does not arrive before you do," Mrs. Bryant said. "You will note, Miss Bray, that we endeavour to be extremely efficient in our arrangements just as we try to provide our clients with only the best type of servant in every category."

"I appreciate that," Tatika said, "and thank you. I will call tomorrow morning."

She curtseyed politely to Mrs. Bryant, then walked quickly out into Mount Street.

Ellen was waiting for her at the entrance to Mudies' Lending Library. Tatika put her arms round her and kissed her on the cheek.

"I am employed, Ellen! I have found a job! I am leaving on Friday!"

"I don't believe it," Ellen retorted. "They've never taken you as a companion, Miss Tatika."

"They have and I am going to Scotland," Tatika said. "At least there I will be well out of the way of Lord Crowley and Step-mama. They will never think to look for me so far away."

"I beg of you, Miss Tatika, not to do anything so

crazy," Ellen pleaded. "I never thought for a moment that anything would come of this wild idea of your being a companion. Companion indeed! What would your mother say?"

"I think Mama would have thought it was a grand joke," Tatika replied. "You remember how she used to laugh when we dressed up to amuse Papa or frighten you almost into hysterics when we pretended to be ghosts!"

"This is a pretence, Ellen. I shall be acting a part simply because it will save me from something so unpleasant, so horrid that if Mama were here, I know she would help me to run away."

"If your mother was here there would be no cause for running," Ellen said bitterly.

"That is true," Tatika agreed with a sigh. "But sometimes I feel she is close to me. Last night when I went to bed I knew as surely as if I had heard her say it, she did not wish me to marry Lord Crowley."

She was telling the truth and not saying so merely to influence Ellen. But she knew that it would carry great weight with the old maid who had adored her mother and who believed that the Russians often had uncanny powers of clairvoyance.

She was right. Ellen was now prepared to help her.

"You will want all your clothes, Miss Tatika," she said in a practical voice.

"Of course," Tatika answered. "On £50 a year I shall not be able to buy any more. I must take everything I possess with me. How can we get them out of the house?"

"I'll manage it somehow," Ellen replied. "There's not many of the staff that would run tittle-tattling to Her Ladyship, except for that snooty maid of hers whom I never could abide."

There was an endless battle between Ellen and Lady Lynch's French Lady's maid who was called Marie.

The two women hated each other, and if Marie

could strike at Ellen through Tatika there was no doubt she would do so.

"Do not worry," Ellen said. "The footmen are decent boys and if I ask them to carry down the baggage and say nothing about it they'll do it for me."

"We will have to give some sort of excuse for so many trunks leaving the house," Tatika said.

"I shall say you are giving some of your old clothes to a charity which helps retired actresses," Ellen said. "I believe there is one."

"No, I know of a better story than that," Tatika said. "When Grand-mama died, if you remember, Ellen, her clothing was sent to The Society for Distressed Gentlefolk."

"Of course," Ellen said, "I remember now."

"Tell the footmen you have been sorting out some of my things I have not worn for a long time. You need not pack my ball-dresses anyway."

"You will take everything with you that's worth wearing," Ellen said sharply. "As you have said, on £50 a year you'll not be able to afford any of the grand gowns that you're wearing now, and what is more I shall not be there to press them for you!"

This was a cry that Tatika had been anticipating.

"As soon as I can think clearly and feel I am not being forced into a marriage with Lord Crowley, I shall begin to plan for the future."

"'And I can be with you?" Ellen asked.

"How do you think I could possibly be without you?" Tatika answered. "Dear Ellen, apart from Papa, you are the only person I love in the world, and wherever I go, wherever I am, I want you to be with me. What will you do when I have left?"

"I shall go and stay with my sister in Worthing," Ellen said. "She keeps a small boarding-house and I always meant to retire there when I was too old to work."

"That will not be for years and years!" Tatika said. "Go to your sister, give me the address, and very shortly, Ellen, perhaps in a few months, we will be together."

Her mind leapt ahead and she said:

"Once I have impressed some publisher with my qualifications I am sure I can make money for us to have a tiny place of our own! Perhaps at first it will only be one room. It would be fun to live in Edinburgh, I am told it is a very beautiful city."

"I will not have you going to Edinburgh alone," Ellen said fiercely. "If it is a question of looking for rooms I will go there first and you can join me."

Tatika gave a little laugh.

"I promise you I will be very careful with myself! Quite frankly I am not afraid of anything or anybody except Lord Crowley."

"You are too young to know all the dangers of this wicked world," Ellen said.

"I have encountered quite a number already," Tatika answered. "Do you remember that Count in Rome who pursued me when I was only fifteen? I held him at bay with one of Papa's duelling swords, and he really thought I was going to kill him!"

"You may not be so fortunate on another occasion," Ellen said gloomily.

"And there was that tiresome Baron in Austria," Tatika went on, "who was reputed to have dozens of illegitimate children, most of whom were much older than I. But that did not stop him from trying to climb up to my bed-room window at night."

"In the past you've always had your Papa to run to in an emergency," Ellen said, "and I've been with you too. But this time, my dearie, you'll be on your own! I'll never sleep at nights a'worrying about you."

"I will write to you at Worthing to say how dull, how quiet, how quite uneventful Scotland is," Tatika laughed. "And now, Ellen, we have to be busy. You have only tomorrow in which to pack everything and I am sure it would be wise if you could take some of the trunks tomorrow and put them in the Left Luggage Office at Euston Station."

"I'll do that," Ellen agreed.

Tatika considered for a moment before she said:

"And you must leave on the same day as I do, Ellen. I will not have her bullying you! Besides, she might frighten you into telling her where I am!"

"Do you really think I would betray you?" Ellen asked.

Regardless of the fact that they were turning into Berkeley Square, Tatika kissed her old maid on the cheek.

"I am only teasing," she said. "I know you would be hung, drawn, quartered and burned at the stake rather than betray me! That is why I trust you, Ellen, and also why I love you."

They arrived back at Charles Street to find there was a note for Tatika. She knew as she saw the flamboyant coronet on the back of the envelope who it was from. She opened it and read:

> I will call for you at noon, my valiant little Fighter. Do not refuse to accompany me in the Park, otherwise I must ask your Step-mother to intercede on my behalf. I am anxious to see you.

> Crowley.

The note was characteristic of him, Tatika thought bitterly. He not only commanded her to obey him, but he threatened her.

He knew, because she had told him so exactly what treatment she would receive from her Step-mother should she refuse to do what he requested.

"He is despicable," she said aloud as she went upstairs to change her gown.

Lord Crowley arrived in an elegant open Victoria drawn by two magnificent horses and attended by servants wearing a blue and yellow livery and high cockaded top-hats.

His entourage was undoubtedly smarter than any other to be seen on Rotten Row.

"I have arranged with your father that I shall send a notice of our engagement to the London *Gazette* and the daily newspapers," Lord Crowley told her.

"Ask them to insert it on Monday," Tatika said.

"Why then?" he enquired.

"I always feel that Friday is an unlucky day for engagements to be announced," Tatika replied, "and on Saturday many people are in the country and some might miss such an important item of news."

The irony in her voice dispersed his suspicion that she might be wishing to postpone the announcement.

"Then Monday if it pleases you," he conceded.

"I am afraid I have many superstitions."

"That is to be expected," he answered, "so I will not ask you to sit down thirteen at our wedding breakfast, marry me on a Friday, or turn the mattresses on that day of the week."

He laughed and added:

"Those are the Prince of Wales' superstitions. No mattress at Marlborough House is ever turned on a Friday."

"And of course we must all follow the lead of the Heir to the Throne," Tatika said.

"Are you afraid that I shall be as unfaithful to you as he is to Princess Alexandra?" Lord Crowley asked.

"Would I have any say in the matter?" Tatika enquired.

"As you have no choice whether to marry me or not," Lord Crowley replied, "the answer is of course none."

"You are very sure of getting what you want," Tatika remarked.

"As I told you at the beginning of our acquaintance, you are very desirable and I want you more violently than I can tell you at this moment when we are being watched by so many curious eyes," Lord Crowley replied.

There was a sudden passion in his voice which made Tatika feel as if he opened the doors of a fiery furnace and she felt the heat reaching out to scorch her.

"There are so many other women in the world," she said quietly.

"Millions of them," Lord Crowley agreed, "but only one that looks like you, only one who is prepared to oppose me, try to evade me, and whom I am determined to conquer."

"And will that make you happy," Tatika asked, "knowing that I dislike you, that I hate you to touch me, that I would escape you if I could?"

"I think your resistance is the most exciting thing I have ever encountered," Lord Crowley said. "Women have after a while always bored me. But I have never failed to enjoy the stalk, the pursuit, the chase, the hunt and the kill!"

His voice was mocking as he added:

"Where you are concerned, Tatika, I feel it will be a very long time before I reach the stage of boredom which comes from satiation."

Tatika drew in her breath. She longed to defy him, she longed to tell him that she was not an animal to be trapped and tortured, just to satisfy what she knew was a perverted lust within him.

Then she knew that nothing she could say would make the slightest difference. There was only one thing she could do and she had already decided to do it.

They had driven down the whole length of the Row and by now the carriage was in the less populated and less fashionable part of the Park near the Serpentine.

"Give me your hand," Lord Crowley said suddenly.

"Why?" Tatika asked.

"Because I have asked you to do so," he said with a note of authority in his voice.

"I have no wish for you to touch me."

"But I wish to touch you," he answered. "Do as you are told, Tatika, or I will make you obey me."

She hesitated a moment.

Then telling herself once again it was of no consequence what she did today, she put out her hand abruptly and held it stiffly as he took it in both of his.

She was wearing long, pale grey suede gloves and now he undid the six pearl buttons at the wrists and very slowly drew the glove from her fingers.

She held herself rigid, determined that he should evoke no obvious reaction by what he was doing.

Then as he lifted her hand to his mouth and pressed his warm lips passionately against her palm, she could not prevent a shiver from running through her.

She knew without looking at him that it thrilled him. Then she felt his mouth against her wrists lingering on the softness of her skin.

She knew as he did so he had an intense satisfaction in knowing that she was finding it more and more difficult to refrain from snatching her hand away from him.

"One day, little Tatika," he said in a caressing voice, "I will teach you not to shiver and shrink from me, but to quiver with desire when I hold you close in my arms and my lips touch your skin."

It was as if he had finally goaded her into losing her self-control!

Because she could not help it, Tatika snatched her hand from his and not really realising what she was doing, rubbed with her other hand the place on her wrist where he had kissed her.

"It will not rub away," he said mockingly. "And soon I will kiss you all over your lovely body so that it will be impossible for you to erase my love!"

"I hate you," Tatika said. "Have you forgotten that I hate you?"

"You have challenged me," Lord Crowley replied. "A challenge that I find so irresistible, so exciting, Tatika, that I find myself thinking of you every moment of the day, while I ache agonisingly for you during the long hours of the night."

The manner in which he was speaking and the suggestion behind his words revolted Tatika to the point of nausea.

She clenched her hands together striving to keep calm, knowing it would give him great satisfaction if she became hysterical or if she cried out as her feelings demanded.

She realised now that Lord Crowley, being a sophisticated and experienced man of the world supported by wealth and rank, had been able to seduce almost any woman he desired quite easily into his bed!

That was why her defiance and opposition had aroused him, perhaps in a manner he had never experienced before.

She understood what he meant when he said he wanted to conquer her, to subdue her and triumph in victory over her subjection.

She was certain that he would stop at no cruelty to satisfy his lust or to force her into admitting he was her master.

He was also confident of his own prowess as a lover, certain that sooner or later she would succumb to his attractions, and then undoubtedly he would be bored with her!

Until she did so, he would stalk her as a huntsman stalks a wild animal. Only when she was prostrate at his feet, when she had no fight left in her, would the blazing desire within him be assuaged.

They drove on and after a little while Tatika found her panic was subsiding, she was no longer trembling.

She put on her glove again, doing up the pearl buttons, aware that Lord Crowley was watching her. But he made no further effort to touch her.

The horses had turned for home.

"Will you dine with me tonight?" he asked.

"Would not tomorrow do just as well?" she asked. "I have a headache and as you well know we have been out three nights running."

"If I let you off this evening," he asked, "will you reward me for my consideration?"

"It depends on what that is," Tatika answered cautiously.

"I wish to dance with you again," Lord Crowley said. "I like the feeling of your body moving against mine. I think it would be amusing to have a small party at Crowley House tomorrow night. We will announce our engagement to our immediate friends and I think your Step-mother would be pleased to meet the Prince of Wales if he can be present."

"I am sure she would be overjoyed," Tatika said with a sarcastic note in her voice.

"And you?"

"I shall of course be honoured to meet His Royal Highness."

"That is not what I was asking you," Lord Crowley said. "I was really wanting to know if you would enjoy the party at which we would tell a very select number of my personal friends that you had promised to be my wife."

"A promise that was extorted from me."

"Not at the point of a pistol," Lord Crowley mocked, "but by the threat of the whip! A very effective weapon, Tatika!"

"I have suggested before," Tatika answered, "that you should be man enough to fight your own battles."

He smiled.

"Are you really questioning my manhood? That I assure you, little Tatika, is something I can prove all too easily."

He saw a faint flush rise in her cheeks at the coarseness of his words and he laughed.

"You are adorable!" he said. "So adorable that I am really being considerate and unselfish in waiting until tomorrow night before I kiss your lips again."

Chapter Five

"I've escaped! I'm free! "Tatika cried to herself.

And the wheels of the train seemed to be repeating the words over and over again, "free—free—free."

She had feared up to the very last moment that she would be prevented from leaving.

She was sure her Step-mother would somehow find out that her trunks were being moved out of the house, or by some terrible coincidence Lord Crowley would be standing at Euston Station as she and Ellen arrived.

When he had kissed her hand in Hyde Park and told her that he intended to kiss her lips the following night, she had known she could bear no more!

It would be impossible for her to go to Crowley House, to dance with him, to know that he was manoeuvering so that they could be alone, and she would once again feel the lewd possessiveness of his mouth.

She had reached breaking-point. It was impossible to go on acting a part even though she knew the way of escape was planned for the day after tomorrow.

As Lord Crowley drove her back to Charles Street she had said:

"Could we stop at a Stationer's? I promised my

Step-mother that I would buy her the latest copy of *The Ladies Journal*."

"Of course," Lord Crowley replied and gave the order to the footman on the box.

"Let the man get it for you," he suggested as the horses came to a standstill.

"There is a magazine I need myself," Tatika replied, "but unfortunately I have forgotten the name."

She stepped out, leaving him in the carriage. Inside the stationer's she asked for *The Ladies Journal* and also Bradshaw's monthly Railway and Steamer Navigation Guide. It cost 6d.

She concealed it in her recticule and went back to the carriage.

"The magazine I required has not yet been issued," she explained.

It was only a short distance to Charles Street, yet even in the few minutes it took to drive there she found herself shrinking once again from the close proximity of Lord Crowley.

She had run upstairs to her bed-room to find Ellen sorting out her clothes and arranging them on the bed.

"I hope Her Ladyship does not see you!" Tatika exclaimed.

"Even if she did she wouldn't be suspicious," Ellen replied. "I should tell her I'm tidying out the room and taking the things you don't need upstairs."

She dropped her voice and added:

"That's where I'm packing, in my own bed-room! It's not likely the New Mistress will visit me there."

Tatika took the Bradshaw's Guide out of her reticule.

"'Our plans have changed, Ellen," she said. "I am leaving tomorrow instead of Friday."

"I can't have everything ready by then!" Ellen exclaimed.

"You have to!" Tatika replied. "I cannot go to Crowley House tomorrow as His Lordship intends.

He is giving a dinner party with a dance afterwards, and he is going to invite the Prince of Wales."

"Surely then, it would be wiser to leave the following day," Ellen protested.

"No," Tatika said firmly. "I have told you, Ellen, that I cannot bear it. I cannot endure him any longer!"

She was turning over the pages of Bradshaw's Guide as she spoke.

"There is a train leaving for Glasgow at four o'clock tomorrow afternoon," she said, "which arrives at five o'clock the following morning."

"That's too early!" Ellen protested. "Glasgow is a big city, Miss Tatika, and you should not be alone there unchaperoned. Heaven knows what might happen to you!"

"Nothing will happen," Tatika answered, "because if the train is punctual I see that I can catch a Steamer which leaves for Inverness at six o'clock that morning. I am sure you would rather that I slept on the steamer than in Glasgow."

"I don't like to think of you travelling anywhere alone," Ellen answered sharply. "Let me come with you, Miss Tatika. I'll pay my own fare."

"Certainly not!" Tatika replied. "You want all the money you have to keep yourself while you are with your sister until we can be together again."

"I thought it would be wise, when you leave, Miss Tatika, to tell the household that I've had a letter to say my sister is ill," Ellen said.

"You had best not say she lives in Worthing," Tatika remarked.

Then she gave a little cry.

"I have a splendid idea, Ellen! You will tell the staff that your sister lives in Crewe, and that will give us an excuse to go to Euston. I will say I am going with you to see you off, and no-one will think it strange."

She returned to her perusal of Bradshaw's Guide.

"Of course the train may be late, the boat may

not start, all sorts of things may happen," she said. "I must have enough money with me for emergencies. How can we contrive that?"

"I'll lend you some," Ellen suggested.

"You know I would not take it," Tatika replied. "Let me think."

She was silent for a moment, then she said:

"Papa always keeps some money in the drawer in his Dressing-room. To help myself seems rather like stealing but at the same time I shall be no expense to him in the future."

"Oh, Miss Tatika, don't talk as if you're planning to be away for the rest of your life!" Ellen cried. "The Master'll miss you once you have gone. He's always loved you, it's only this cruel, wicked woman who has tried to poison his mind against you."

"Yes I know that," Tatika said, "and I shall write Papa a letter and hide it under my pillow. The housemaids will not find it until we are far away."

"I'm sure I can't get everything finished by tomorrow," Ellen grumbled.

"Well, what you cannot pack must be left behind," Tatika retorted.

As she spoke she knew that Ellen would somehow get everything done in time.

Sure enough, three of her trunks were taken to Euston Station that very evening, which left only one large one and some hand luggage for her and Ellen to take the following day.

They made their plans very carefully, and while Tatika was having a light luncheon with her Stepmother, she said:

"I thought if you did not want me, Step-mama, I would lie down this afternoon. I feel rather tired and I think perhaps I have a cold coming."

"If this is the prelude for an excuse not to come to the party this evening, you can forget it," Lady Lynch snapped.

Tatika opened her eyes wide.

"I had not thought of such a thing," she said. "Besides I believe the Prince of Wales will be there."

Lady Lynch gave a sigh of satisfaction.

"So Lord Crowley told me in his note of invitation. I am very much looking forward to meeting His Royal Highness."

"I thought you had already met him on several occasions," Tatika said.

"I have been presented, but we have not had an intimate conversation," Lady Lynch replied. "This will be different, very different, Tatika. Tonight you will realise what a very lucky girl you are."

There was no mistaking the jealousy in her tone and when Tatika did not answer she said:

"I hope you have got over your airs and graces and are going to behave sensibly in future. If you do not, you will find that my threat of a beating still stands."

"I had not forgotten," Tatika murmured in a low voice.

"You would be very foolish to do so," Lady Lynch said menacingly.

She rose from the Dining-room table.

"Go to bed now," she said, "and try to look pleased to see Lord Crowley when you meet him. Even a man in love can get bored with a sullen face, however pretty it may be."

"I will do my best," Tatika answered meekly.

Lady Lynch glanced at her Step-daughter as if she was suspicious of this new conciliatory manner. Then she shrugged her shoulders.

"For my part," she said, "I cannot think why he wants to marry you. But then there is no fool like an old fool!"

She flounced from the room in front of Tatika, who slipped quickly upstairs to where Ellen was waiting for her in her bed-room.

She changed into a travelling-dress and cloak of dark sapphire-blue alpaca and put on her head a little bonnet from which she had removed all the superfluous trimmings and tied the ribbons under her chin.

"Do I look like a companion?" she asked Ellen gayly.

"You look very beautiful, my dearie," Ellen replied. "Oh, Miss Tatika, don't do it! Don't go on with this ridiculous idea! You'll be Queen of Society, you will be moving in the circles to which you were born, you'll be feted and admired! How can you possibly prefer to be what is no more than a superior servant."

"I prefer anything to marrying His Lordship!" Tatika declared. "Come, Ellen, it is too late for regrets, let us escape while we can. Is the luggage downstairs?"

"It's at the back-door, Miss. The staff are all having their lunch now that you and Her Ladyship have finished. If we slip down the backstairs we can find a hackney cab and no-one will realise we've left."

"Did you tell the housemaids I was going to lie down and did not wish to be disturbed?"

"I told them that before luncheon," Ellen said. "If they see you leaving, we can say you have changed your mind. But it's my belief that with a little luck no-one'll notice us."

"Come on then," Tatika urged.

She picked up a large leather handbag into which she had put the ticket she had collected that morning from the Domestic Agency, the money she had taken from her father's drawer, and the £4 that Mrs. Bryant had given her for the journey.

She had not told Mrs. Bryant she was leaving that afternoon, but she had herself sent a telegram from the Post Office in Mount Street to Mr. Torquill McCraig at the Castle.

> Miss Bray with excellent testimonial leaving for Scotland today. Confident she will prove suitable for position and fulfil your requirements.
>
> Bryant Domestic Bureau

There were also in Tatika's bag the labels for her trunks which she intended to tie on as soon as they reached Euston Station.

She and Ellen were fortunate. A hackney cab was driving past just as Ellen reached the back-door. He was an obliging cabby and lifted their luggage onto the roof without taking too long about it.

Tatika slipped inside the cab and Ellen followed her, shutting the back-door of the house behind her.

"We have got away!" Tatika exclaimed breathlessly as the cab drove down the street and into Berkeley Square.

"I hope so," Ellen said apprehensively.

It was not until the train actually steamed out of the station leaving Ellen in tears on the platform that Tatika really felt safe.

Then she settled herself in a corner of her carriage, which was marked "Ladies Only" and felt a wave of relief flow over her.

"I'm free! I'm free!"

Free from Lord Crowley, free from her Stepmother's threats, free in a way she had never been free before in the whole of her life.

She was not apprehensive about travelling alone. She had travelled a great deal over the continent with either her father or her governess.

She did not feel agitated, as some people were, on railway stations. She was quite philosophical about missing a train or a ship, knowing there would be another one later, which would serve her purpose just as well.

At the same time this was the first occasion on which she had ever been completely alone and would, during the whole journey, have to fend for herself.

There would be no Aide-de-Camp from an Embassy to meet her at Glasgow or at Inverness. There would be no smart private carriage to carry her to her destination, and when she did arrive at the Castle she would have to behave with humility, something she had certainly never attempted before.

"It is a real adventure," Tatika thought.

She found herself recalling the Vikings and what an adventure it had been for them to set off to raid or conquer an unknown land with the possibility of being killed, wounded or captured.

She hoped there would be a Library at the Castle, so that perhaps she could continue the studies she had started at the British Museum. There was so much more she wanted to know, so much she wanted to learn!

She thought of the narrow wooden boats riding over the waves, the Viking Chiefs wearing their horned helmets, their vivid blue eyes searching the horizon for enemy ships and their first sight of land.

She imagined a Viking Chief making love to her. He would be young with a strong, muscular body, not soft from over-luxurious living like Lord Crowley.

He would kiss her hand and then her lips, and she would thrill to his touch instead of being repelled and disgusted!

She day-dreamed in this manner and had no interest in opening the magazines which lay beside her on the seat, before the train reached Crewe.

Ellen had carefully packed a small wicker basket with food for the journey. But Tatika realised she would need something to drink, and following the majority of other passengers on the train she went in search of a Buffet.

It took her some time to get a cup of tea and, when she had drunk it and been to the Ladies' Waiting Room to wash her hands, it was almost time for the train to start again.

She went back to her carriage. Since leaving London she had been the only occupant, but now she found four other women had moved in during her absence.

She looked at them and for a moment felt embarrassed, thinking they were the type she had seen walking the streets of Rome or Vienna.

They had bright rouged cheeks and very red lips, their eye lashes were heavily mascaraed and the hair of two of the women was dyed gold so blatantly as to be almost blinding.

But as Tatika seated herself in the corner where she had deposited her wicker luncheon-basket, she realised that her fellow travellers were in fact actresses.

It was quite easy to read the boldly printed labels on their luggage which was piled on the racks over their heads.

"Stage Door, the Caledonian Theatre, Glasgow," was inscribed on every label and the woman sitting opposite Tatika smiled.

"If you're curious about us, we are just as curious about you," she said. "It is quite a coincidence that you're travelling to Castle Craig."

She looked up at the label on Tatika's hand-baggage as she spoke.

"Do you know the Castle?" Tatika asked.

"I should say we do! We all went there for two nights last year when we had finished our time in Glasgow. It was fun, wasn't it, Gwen?"

She spoke to the woman sitting next to her who had the gaudily golden hair that Tatika had noticed on entering the carriage.

"It was fun all right for a week-end," Gwen answered, "but I wouldn't care to stay there long. The place gave me the willies!"

"Are you a friend of the Duke?" the woman opposite Tatika asked curiously.

"I am taking the position of companion to the Dowager Duchess of Strathcraig," Tatika answered, "Do tell me about her."

The woman called Gwen shrieked with laughter.

"You don't suppose we were allowed to meet any Duchesses!" she cried. "Not on your life. It was the gentlemen who entertained us. My! If ever there was a good looker, it's the Duke! But Angie'll tell you about him."

Angie, who was the woman sitting opposite Tatika, looked coy.

"Well, he was certainly what you'd expect a Duke to be like," she told Tatika. "I hope he asks us again this year, especially as you're going to be there."

"I have never been to Scotland before," Tatika said, "so do tell me all about it."

"There's not a lot to tell," Gwen interposed before Angie could speak. "It's cold, hellish uncomfortable and—are they dour. Try to get a laugh out of some of the audiences and it's worse than extracting a winkle without a pin."

"Oh it's not as bad as all that," Angie expostulated, "but you see we usually open a new play in Glasgow, and then after Edinburgh come gradually South until we get to London. One always feels a bit on edge when the play's new and don't know your lines as well as you ought to! Eh, Rosie?"

She gave a glance at one of the other girls who was sitting in the carriage beyond Tatika.

"Don't talk about it!" Rosie groaned. "I never can remember my lines until we've been going at least three weeks."

"That's the truth if you never say another word," Gwen exclaimed. "I'm fed up with having to learn your part as well as my own!"

"What is your play called?" Tatika asked.

"*Pretty Polly Peckham*," Angie replied. "It's a comedy. I play the lead."

She was very pretty in a flamboyant manner and Tatika thought she certainly had much more animation and personality than the other three women.

She also had a very good figure and Tatika could understand that men would find her attractive—even the good-looking Duke who seemed to command the admiration of everyone he met.

"Please tell me more about the Castle," she begged.

"You'll not like it—not for long," Angie said positively. "Of course if the Duke should take a fancy to you that'll be a different matter. But there's something creepy about the whole place. He didn't say anything, of course. I just felt in my bones there was something rather sinister about the whole set-up."

"It's only because you didn't like Torquill McCraig," Gwen accused. "I thought he was a real dasher, and he certainly wasn't slow in coming forward."

The other women laughed.

"Go on, Gwen, you always lose your heart to anyone who pays you so much as a compliment," Rosie said. "That Torquill McCraig was not really interested in you. He never came to see the show when we opened in Edinburgh, and I didn't see many bunches of flowers from him in your Dressing-room."

"We only played in Edinburgh for a fortnight," Gwen said. "I'll bet you we hear from him again this year."

"How will he know we are there?" Rosie asked.

"Because I wrote and told him so," Gwen said defiantly. "So there!"

Angie laughed.

"Oh well, it seems as though we shall be seeing you after all," she said to Tatika. "If Gwen has set her heart on a thing—or should I say a man—there's no holding her."

"It's all practice, my dear," Gwen sniggered.

"I was thinking of taking the steamer from Glasgow to Inverness," Tatika said.

"That's the best way," Angie agreed. "Let me see, we reached Inverness about two o'clock in the afternoon, and then it was about a two hour's drive to the Castle. But of course the Duke sent a carriage with two horses for us."

"I do not expect to be so grand," Tatika said with a smile.

"You know, you're ever so pretty," Angie said. "Why don't you go on the stage? It'ld be a great deal more fun than being a companion, whatever that may mean."

"I am sure it would be," Tatika agreed, "but I don't expect I have any talent for acting."

As she spoke she thought with a quiet smile to herself that she was not doing too badly.

"If you ask me, you'ld be a smash!" Gladys said. "If you made up your eyelashes with mascara and put some lip salve on your mouth you'd soon have Angie wanting to scratch your eyes out with jealousy."

"I would not want that," Tatika smiled. "So perhaps I had better stay as I am."

"If you change your mind, come and see me some time and I'll try to help you," Angie said generously.

"That is very kind of you," Tatika answered, "but I have found myself a job that I think will suit me for the time being at any rate."

"Well, don't let them work you too hard," Gwen said. "I've always heard that ladies like Duchesses give themselves terrible airs and grind their wretched servants into the dust."

"Didn't we do a play with a Duchess in it once?" Rosie asked.

"Yes, of course we did!" Angie said. "That was the one in which you were the injured wife."

Rosie made a face.

"Oh, it was a rotten part! I don't want to do that again."

"It wasn't a success," Angie said briefly. "I prefer the type of comedy we are doing now."

"I hate comedy," Rosie announced, "and I'll never know my lines."

She got a manuscript out of her bag and started reading. She was the least attractive of the four women, Tatika thought.

Angie was chatting away about the Glasgow audiences, the lodgings at which they stayed which grew more uncomfortable every year, and a row she had had with the Stage Manager.

Tatika found herself puzzling over the fact that these actresses had been asked to Castle Craig.

Somehow it seemed out of keeping with everything she had expected. It certainly did not seem to fit in with the previous companions' complaints of loneliness and isolation.

It also seemed to her strange that the Duke of Strathcraig, who must be of tremendous importance in the social world, should wish to associate with these rather cheap and common types of women.

"I do not understand," Tatika thought to herself.

She found, however, that Angie and her companions certainly helped the long railway journey to pass quickly, as they chattered away until the early hours of the morning.

Then after they had slept somewhat fitfully, they roused themselves as dawn was breaking to apply more make-up to their faces and got themselves ready for the train's arrival at Glasgow Station.

"I'll tell you one thing," Angie said, "I'm going straight to bed! If they call a rehearsal before noon, I'm not attending it."

"Oh, he wouldn't do that, would he," Rosie wailed. "I haven't had a chance to learn my lines."

"I wouldn't put anything past him," Gwen said. "If ever there was a Stage Manager that I really dislike, it's this one."

With the expression of many good wishes and hopes that they would meet again, Angie and the others said goodbye to Tatika.

The train had hardly come to a stop before Tatika hurried out of the carriage and finding a porter persuaded him with the promise of a large tip to extract her luggage from the van and find her a cab.

"Where be ye a'going, Ma'am?" he asked.

"I want to take the Steamer that leaves at six o'clock for Inverness," Tatika explained.

"I ken we'll do it, Ma'am," he said cheerily, and his optimism was not unjustified.

Tatika caught *The Maid of Morven* with fifteen minutes to spare.

The dull grey dawn had turned to rain and she

was thankful to find that by expending twenty shillings she could have a seat in the cabin.

The majority of passengers were not so opulent and huddled on deck striving to find protection against the wind and rain from the super-structure.

Tatika had learned from Bradshaw's Guide that they travelled by the Crinan Canal to Oban, on to Fort William, Corpach and the Caledonian Canal to Inverness.

She looked forward to steaming right across Scotland to the East coast. But unfortunately the weather worsened and, though she rose many times from her seat to look out of the windows, there was little to see but sheets of beating rain.

Because she was tired, Tatika felt the high spirits in which she had started her journey had evaporated and now she felt depressed and lonely.

At least the chatter and good humour of Angie and her companions had been preferable to the stiff reserve of the passengers on *The Maid of Morven* who obviously had no wish to converse with her.

The women among them eyed her smart travelling get-up with suspicion or resentment.

"Have I made a mistake after all?" Tatika asked herself and then knew she was being over-sensitive and too easily cast down.

Lowering herself a little in her seat she shut her eyes and because she was in fact very tired, she dozed on and off.

Food of a sort was available on board but Tatika found some sandwiches and breast of chicken were still left in her wicker picnic-basket. However she bought a bowl of soup and later several cups of tea.

A large number of passengers got off en route and few people made the whole journey.

In the half-empty cabin, Tatika found it easy to sleep comparatively well, although she longed to change her clothes and wished she had been brave enough to stay the night at a hotel in Glasgow.

But when finally the Steamer hooting noisily

reached Inverness, she found herself rested and full of energy and excitedly anticipating what lay ahead.

Perhaps because she looked smart and certainly more attractive than any of the other passengers she immediately found a porter to carry her luggage ashore. But when she asked how she could travel from Inverness to Castle Craig he scratched his head.

"'Tis tae late tae take the coach," he said. "But auld Sandy travels tae Castle Craig on a Saturday. He may hae left, but I doot it. I heard from somewan this morn he wae a'having repairs done tae th' wheel of his cart."

"Who is Sandy?" Tatika asked.

"He be th' Carrier," the porter answered. "Come away, Ma'am, we'll be seeing if we can find him."

It was quite a walk to where apparently Sandy was to be found, and the porter pushing his truck moved so quickly that Tatika had difficulty in keeping up with him.

Finally they ran Sandy to ground just as he was about to set off in his open cart. He was in fact actually climbing into it when the porter hailed him.

"Hi Sandy!" he shouted, "wait a-while, mon, I hae a passenger for ye."

Sandy was an old man with white hair and a long moustache, wearing a tattered and dilapidated kilt.

He had a moth-eaten bonnet on the side of his head and a coat which looked as if the rats had been at it. But he was quite willing to take Tatika as a passenger.

"It'll give ma a wee bit of company, Lass," he said. " 'Tis quite a step to th' Castle."

"Ye not be a'coming hame this night?" the Porter asked.

"Nay, I'll stay the Sabbath with ma wife's father's sister who lives oop the Glen," Sandy answered.

The two men helped Tatika into the high cart. Her baggage was piled up behind and many of the goods that Sandy carried had to be moved to make way for them.

There was certainly a mixed collection under an old tarpaulin.

There was a live cockerel in a cage. There was a very ancient sewing-machine which Tatika guessed had been to Inverness for repair, and there were bags and boxes, tins and cases which she supposed contained the many varied objects required by the servants in a big house.

Tatika had not managed her father's residences for many years without learning that the servants liked to spend a few pence or even shillings every week out of their wages.

Where a house was in the country or outside a town, there was invariably a carrier to collect the goods required or bring for their perusal tempting rolls of ribbons, wools or silks to be fingered over and argued about.

The carrier's arrival at any large house was the main excitement of the week.

Tatika herself had often made use of a carrier's services, when she required a special coloured ribbon, a few yards of silk to line a dress, or perhaps some buttons for a new blouse.

It was Ellen who had explained to her how the system worked, and as she set off on her journey at Sandy's side she asked him if all the goods he carried were intended for the Castle.

"Most o' 'em," he answered. "Th' cock be for th' wifie of the Head Forester, and the sewing machine be the personal property of the Mither of the second Stalker."

"I am lucky you were leaving today," Tatika said.

"Aye," he answered, "I'm usually awa' soon after noon, but t'will nae take us long if we goes o'er the moor."

"Are there two roads?" Tatika asked, remembering that Angie had said it had taken an hour and a half in the Duke's carriage.

"Aye, there be the new road," Sandy answered, "with a reel fine surface fae them as goes tae Dormach an the north. But old Bessie kens her way o'er th' hill and we can cut off tae miles."

The rain that had obscured the landscape while the Steamer was passing through the Canal had now cleared.

In the morning there had been no sunshine, but now the sun came out, and as soon as they were clear of the town, Tatika had her first glimpse of Scotland in all its beauty.

There were the moors rising higher and higher, not yet purple with the heather still a soft green and there was the sea deepening in colour as it stretched away towards the horizon.

"It is lovely!" Tatika exclaimed. "Just as lovely as I expected it to be!"

"Aye, it be a grand country," Sandy said. "Will ye be staying lang?"

There was no mistaking his curiosity and Tatika smiled as she answered.

"I hope so, I am to be a companion to the Dowager Duchess."

"Her Grace be a fine Lady," Sandy said, "an' the late Duke were a great man. Verry respected he wae."

"Have you lived here all your life?" Tatika asked.

"Aye an' ma people afore me," Sandy answered. "I'm a McCraig as be most o' them who dwell here abouts."

"Are the McCraigs a big Clan?" Tatika asked.

"'Tis said we be spread o'er the world," Sandy replied, "and we've followed our Chiefs wherever they hae led us."

He chuckled as he added:

"If ye be a'staying in the Castle, ye hae better be looking oot for the ghost o' Duke Malcolm?"

"Who was he?" Tatika asked.

"A grand mon, a verry grand mon," Sandy replied. "Ma great grand-father fought beside him in the Rebellion of Forty-Five, and ma grand-father when he wae but a wee lad remembers seeing His Grace."

"I suppose the Duke fought against the English in support of Bonny Prince Charlie," Tatika said.

"Aye," Sandy agreed. "An' those were awfu' hard days, but Duke Malcolm defied th' Sassenachs! They couldna catch him an' do ye know why?"

"No, why?" Tatika asked.

"Because, Lass, he could make himself invisible!" Sandy explained.

"That sounds very strange," Tatika said. "How could anyone make himself invisible?"

"That was the Duke's secret" Sandy said with satisfaction. "Drove th' English mad, he did. They offered a reward of £10,000 to any mon who would bring the Duke to them alive or dead."

"And they still could not catch him?" Tatika asked.

"I've told ye he could make himself invisible," Sandy replied. "They'ld see him laughing at 'em from a window o' the Castle or from the battlements. Yet wheen the soldiers stormed the place he passed through the midst o' them and they couldna see him!"

"It sounds extraordinary," Tatika said, striving to keep the note of incredulity out of her voice. "How do you think the Duke managed it?"

"He had the magic," Sandy answered. "There wae naw doot o' it! He knew how tae defeat the English without even firing a shot at them."

"And they never caught him?"

Sandy shook his head.

"Nay, he died in th' end through treachery. One o' awe own turned traitor."

"Tell me about it," Tatika begged.

"T' wae a McCraig that lived in London an' his mind poisoned wae by the English an' his pocket lined with their gold. The Duke of Cumberland hae given up a'trying tae capture Duke Malcolm an' withdrew his troops."

Sandy chuckled.

"They hae even tried tae burn the Castle but t'was too strong for them. Ye canna burn stone! But there wae a great gathering o' the Clan."

"It must have been some time after the rebellion," Tatika interposed.

"Aye it wae that," Sandy agreed. "Our rightful King had fled to France an' the Scots hae been defeated at Culloden Moor."

There was a sad note in the old man's voice which told Tatika that the humiliation of being defeated by the English was still painful.

"Go on," she begged, "what happened to the Duke?"

"His Grace called the Clan together—what wae left o' them—an' they came into the Castle to pay homage an' declare their loyalty. It wae then the black McCraig struck! When he knelt on one knee in front o' the Duke he hae a dagger hidden under his plaid an' as he rose he thrust it into His Grace's chest."

"It killed him?" Tatika asked.

"Aye, he died the following nicht."

"And what happened to the black McCraig?"

"He was hurled from the window onto the rocks," Sandy said. "But his deed'll e'er be remembered! His ain flesh an' blood moved away because folks wouldna speak with them."

"How do you think the Duke managed to be invisible?" Tatika asked.

"T'was a secret that died with him," Sandy said. "Many hae sought to learn it an' just as many hae failed. He were a grand mon an' we will n'er see his like agin."

Tatika smiled. This was the sort of legend she liked to hear! A legend of Scotland! She was certain there were many of them, and she thought that she must search the Library for more tales like that of Duke Malcolm.

They drove on for some time in silence. Now they were right out on the moorland and lights on the hills ahead were more beautiful than anything Tatika had ever seen before.

The mountains rose steeply on one side of them, the sea was far away to the right over a wide stretch of moorland.

A covey of grouse rose ahead. Tatika saw an eagle hovering high in the sky, holding its wings almost motionless as it sought its prey.

She suddenly felt a strange and exciting elation sweep over her.

Then as the sunshine seemed to intensify and almost to blind her eyes with its radiance, she felt that this was what she had been looking for.

A world free from the horrors and miseries of civilisation, a world unconfined, a world where she could be free!

Free! Free! Free! The words repeated themselves again and again in her heart.

Chapter Six

Bessie pulled the heavy cart slowly up a steep incline and when she reached the top came to a standstill.

"We hae a wee restie here which old Bessie kens well, an' if ye'll excuse me, lass, I'll hae a pull o' ma pipe."

"Of course," Tatika smiled, "and I will stretch my legs."

She climbed down from the cart as she spoke to stand looking at the wonderful view stretching below her over the moor lands to where in the distance she could see the blue and emerald of the sea.

The high hills rose up to the left and beyond in the distance she could see the towers and turrets of what she was sure was the Castle.

With the scene bathed in sunshine and the scent of peat and gorse, she thought that never before had she seen a more lovely sight.

Then as she stood on the rough track looking down she saw almost immediately below her there was a river. Silver in the sunshine it wound its way through a narrow valley towards the sea.

"Have I time to walk down and look at the river?" she asked Sandy.

"Aye, take ye time, Lass," he answered, "I'll ne'er gae without ye."

Lifting her skirts a little, Tatika set off towards the river following the sheep tracks which twisted between the clumps of heather made for easier walking.

She had walked some way when she saw below her there was a man fishing. Even as she noticed him she realised as he raised his rod that he had a fish on his line.

Tatika had often watched her father fishing, but she had never seen a salmon caught!

She hurried now thinking how interesting it would be to see a man land one of the big salmon that she knew were to be found in Highland rivers.

The distance was further than she had thought, and yet when she drew nearer she saw the fish was still being played.

There were a number of large stones in the river which Tatika realised made the fisherman's task more difficult. Then she glanced at the angler and saw that he was a large man wearing a kilt and a bonnet on the side of his head.

He was standing in the water in high rubber boots, but Tatika paid little attention to him, being interested only in the salmon he had hooked which was fighting desperately for its life.

It jumped and she saw as the sunshine glistened on its silver body that it was a large fish weighing perhaps over ten pounds.

Then it was running downstream, the line played out until it checked, and now the fisherman was reeling it in slowly but relentlessly.

He drew the salmon almost up to him, until with a twist of its tail it was away, rushing to the other side of the river and striving to escape behind a large stone.

Again there was the sound of the reel and the salmon was drawn towards its captor.

Its head was up, it was almost ready for the gaff. Then with a last despairing effort to avoid destruction it twisted, turned and managed to get the line round one of the rocks.

Just for a second the line was taut! Then there was a splash: the hook came out of the salmon's mouth and the line went slack in the air.

"Oh how disappointing!" Tatika ejaculated involuntarily.

She had drawn quite near to the bank by this time, and as she spoke the fisherman turned his head sharply having obviously been unaware of her presence.

"You are trespassing," he said. "Get off my land immediately!"

There was something harsh and authoritative in his voice. As he spoke his eyes met Tatika's and she stood quite still looking at him.

He was undoubtedly the most handsome man she had ever seen in her life, but there was a frown on his forehead and the lines were deeply etched from the corner of his nose to his mouth.

There was also something almost ferocious in the glare of his blue eyes, which in their anger were strangely disturbing.

Just for a moment neither of them moved. Then without speaking Tatika turned round and walked back the way she had come.

It seemed a long distance from the river back to Sandy's cart waiting at the top of the brow, but she did not look back, and Sandy having seen her coming had already finished his pipe and climbed back onto his seat.

Tatika pulled herself up beside him, then still not looking in the direction of the fisherman she stared straight ahead as they set off again.

"T'is nae far t' the Castle noo," old Sandy remarked, "and 'tis awe doon-hill."

As they journeyed Tatika felt that the agitation she had felt in being spoken to in so rude a manner was subsiding. At the same time she was apprehensive.

She was sure that the fisherman must have been the Duke.

No other man could be so good-looking, so awe-inspiring, or indeed so authoritative in the manner in which he had spoken to her.

But why, if he were the Duke, was he alone?

Her father had never gone fishing without a gillie to accompany him, to net or gaff his fish and to carry all the gear fishermen seem to require for their sport.

It was the same when he went shooting. There was always a loader, and sometimes two at big shoots, to carry his guns and cartridges.

It seemed incredible that the Duke of Strathcraig, who Tatika knew was a person of tremendous importance in Scotland, should fish alone and indeed should be so unnecessarily rude because she had trespassed upon his land. Or was it rather that she had encroached upon his privacy?

For the first time since she had set off on her journey she felt worried.

If the Duke had taken a dislike to her because she had watched him lose a fish, would he refuse to have her in his household and might she not be sent packing immediately?

They drew nearer to the Castle and now she could see that it was very impressive.

Built on the edge of a bay, its gardens were protected by pine trees, while one part of the Castle itself was built on the very edge of a high cliff.

It had a majesty such as Tatika had never seen before, and she was knowledgeable enough in architecture to realise that the part of the Castle that stood on the cliff was very old.

It must have been there, she thought, that Duke Malcolm had defied the English soldiers, and she could see that the additions which made the Castle so large, were much later in architectural style.

There were many turrets and towers and at the end of a long straight avenue of trees there was a large stone arch through which the cart must pass to reach the front door.

The door itself was formidable. Of heavy oak, studded and hinged with iron, it had a grating through which in the past the defenders of the Castle could look on those who called before they opened the door.

Sandy drew the cart to a standstill.

"Thank you very much for bringing me here," Tatika said. "Will you let me know how much I owe you?"

"That'll gae on the Duke's account, Lass," Sandy replied.

"I would rather pay for myself," Tatika answered proudly and handed him the few shillings he asked for his service.

While she was doing this the door had been opened and she saw a kilted servant looking surprised that the carrier's cart had presumed to come to the front of the Castle.

Then he saw Tatika and the words of rebuke that hovered on his lips were checked as she said quietly:

"I am Miss Bray. I am expected and my luggage is on the cart."

A click of the servant's fingers brought footmen in kilts who lifted down her luggage. When it was deposited inside the door the man-servant, who Tatika knew now must be the Butler, said:

"If you will come this way, Miss, I will take you to Mr. McCraig's office."

He led the way through a large and impressive Hall out of which rose a great stone staircase which Tatika realised must be very old, perhaps as old as the Castle itself.

Mr. McCraig's office was on the ground floor and not far from the front door. The Butler opened the door and Tatika saw a luxuriously furnished room in the centre of which there was an imposing leather-topped desk.

There was a man sitting at it and he raised his head enquiringly as they entered.

"Miss Bray has arrived, Mr. McCraig."

Tatika walked across the room and Mr. McCraig

rose slowly to his feet. Then as Tatika reached him he said in astonishment:

"Are you Miss Bray?"

"I am," Tatika replied. "The Domestic Bureau sent a telegram to announce my arrival."

"I have it," Mr. McCraig said. "But it said they were sending me someone who would fulfil my requirements."

Tatika looked at him. He did not ask her to sit down which she felt was rude and she sensed that his immediate reaction to her was antagonistic.

He was a man of over thirty with a long nose and eyes which she felt were just slightly too close together. He had dark hair brushed back from a square forehead and he was wearing a kilt of the McCraig tartan which she had learned to recognise by now.

"I made it quite clear to the Bureau," he said, "that I required someone middle-aged."

"They had no other applicants on their books at the moment," Tatika explained, "and as I have an excellent reference from my last employer, they felt I would be suitable for the position."

"That is what they say in their telegram," Mr. McCraig said, "but I am afraid, Miss Bray, you are not suitable."

Tatika stared at him, surprised at the abruptness of his tone. Then she said:

"My reference will not have reached you so quickly, but I have a copy of it here in my bag."

She opened her bag as she spoke and drew out a copy she had made of the reference she herself had written.

She held it out to Mr. McCraig, but he did not take it from her.

"I made it absolutely clear in my letter to the Bureau," he said, "that the companion for the Dowager Duchess should be a middle-aged woman. You hardly qualify for that category."

"I hoped that, as I was so experienced the matter

of my age would be considered as comparatively unimportant."

"Nevertheless it is," Mr. McCraig said firmly.

Tatika drew in her breath.

"Are you seriously suggesting that I should return to London without even seeing the Dowager Duchess, who I understand requires my services?"

"A carriage will take you to Inverness," Mr. McCraig said. "You can stay the night at an hotel and catch a steamer tomorrow morning which will convey you to Glasgow. Your expenses of course will be fully paid as they were on your journey up."

"But I want to stay in Scotland," Tatika protested, "and, as I have already told you, there was no-one else available . . . no-one at all."

She paused and added:

"I understood you have had difficulty in the past in finding companions who would not feel this Castle too isolated. I like isolated places."

"I am not prepared to argue the question, Miss Bray," Mr. McCraig said in a cold voice. "You will return to Inverness as soon as I can arrange for a carriage to be brought to the front door."

"I do not know why you should take this attitude," Tatika said, "but I think it is extremely unfair."

Mr. McCraig was just about to reply when a deep voice from behind Tatika asked:

"May I enquire what is unfair?"

She turned round quickly. Standing in the doorway was the man she had last seen in the river losing his fish.

She had not realised he was so tall. He must, she thought, be well over six feet three, and now with his head bare showing his pale gold hair she had to admit that he was breathtakingly handsome.

He moved further into the room and Mr. McCraig, still standing behind the desk, said quickly:

"This need not concern you, Magnus."

"I am interested," the Duke answered.

He looked at Tatika as he spoke. There was now

a look of curiosity in his blue eyes, and she sensed that he had regretted his rudeness to her on the river bank.

"I am Miss Bray," she said before Mr. McCraig could speak. "I understood in London that the Dowager Duchess required a companion, and I have been sent here by Mrs. Bryant's Domestic Bureau because they had no-one more suitable on their books."

"And what is unjust about it?" the Duke said.

"Mr. McCraig tells me I am too young for the post," Tatika said. "They were well aware at the Bureau that he had asked for someone middle-aged, but, as my qualifications were so exceptional, they felt that I might be acceptable to Her Grace."

As she spoke she held out the reference which Mr. McCraig had refused to take from her. The Duke took it and read it, then looked at the man standing silent behind the desk.

"Well, Torquill," he said, "what is amiss with this very glowing testimonial?"

"I think, Magnus, you can leave this matter in my hands," Mr. McCraig replied loftily. "You have always been content for me to manage the Household for you."

"My mother was saying only this morning," the Duke said, "that she hoped that Miss Bray would prove satisfactory. She likes, as you know, to have someone who will read to her and Jeannie for all her good qualities is not very literate."

"I am well aware of that," Mr. McCraig said with an angry note in his voice, "and I promise you that my Aunt shall have a companion when I can procure one."

"But Miss Bray is already here."

"I have already said that she is too young. Do you propose to over-ride my authority in this matter?"

There was no doubt now of the animosity with which Mr. McCraig spoke.

The Duke merely smiled good-humouredly.

"I have no desire to over-ride anything that you do or say, Torquill," he replied, "but on this somewhat delicate question of my mother's companion, I feel that she should be the one to make the decision. I think that the best possible solution to the problem is for me to take Miss Bray up to her room.

"If they do not get on well, then arrangements can be made for Miss Bray to travel south tomorrow. It would be, I think, very inhospitable to turn her away tonight when the Steamer will already have left Inverness."

Tatika realised that the Duke must have heard what was said before he entered the room.

There was a sudden light in her eyes as she looked up at him. The thought of returning to London had been a shock which she had not anticipated.

How could she go back? How could she face her Step-mother's fury at her not attending the party at Crowley House and disappearing for several days and nights?

She would not only be faced with the problem of Lord Crowley all over again, but she would undoubtedly have brought down both her Step-mother's and her father's wrath on Ellen for having aided and abetted her in such an escapade.

She felt that if necessary she would plead with the Duke, beg him on her knees to allow her to stay.

Then as she thought wildly of what she could say or do, she realised he was holding the door open for her and waiting for her to pass through it.

She knew as she moved away from the desk that Torquill McCraig was seething with ill-suppressed fury, and she found it hard to understand why he should mind so much her having the chance of staying on in the Castle.

The Duke led her back into the Hall and now they were climbing the beautiful stone staircase to the first floor. She had not known a man could look so magnificent in a kilt.

"This is the old part of the Castle," he said in a conventional tone.

"I thought it must be," Tatika answered, "it is very impressive."

"And very sturdy," the Duke added. "It has withstood centuries of assault."

"So I learned on my way here," Tatika replied.

They had reached the first floor by this time and Tatika saw through an open door a big Salon.

The Duke appeared to hesitate for a moment before he said:

"Would you like to see the most famous room in the Castle? It was here the original McCraig Chieftans received their followers and it was here Charles Stuart hid for two days when he was hunted by the English. It is always called 'The Chief's Room'."

"I would love to see it," Tatika said eagerly.

He led her into one of the finest rooms she had ever seen.

At one end jutting out from the wall there was a huge medieval chimney-piece of carved and ornamented stone which could hold logs the size of small trees.

All down one side of the room were high gothic-style casements with small panes of glass overlooking the sea.

The walls were half panelled and above the ancient oak carved with intricate patterns hung shields and claymores with which the McCraigs had fought all down the centuries.

It was a very beautiful room and Tatika, moving instinctively towards one of the windows, saw that directly below it swirled the waves of the sea splashing against the rocks.

"It is full of history," she said quickly, "a history I should love to study if I am allowed to stay here."

Her eyes met the Duke's, and it seemed to her as if they spoke wordlessly to each other before he said:

"I want to apologise for my rudeness. I did not realise you were a visitor to the Castle."

"I was sorry that you lost your salmon," Tatika said.

"People come to stare," he went on as if she had not spoken, "and I find it, as you can imagine, intolerable."

There was a violent note in his voice which surprised her. Then he said abruptly:

"Let me take you to my mother. She has not been well lately, she often suffers from bronchitis and the winds a few weeks ago were unexpectedly cold."

They walked down along passages which Tatika could tell led to the newer additions to the Castle.

She could not help being impressed by the pictures, the furniture and the antiquity of everything she saw.

Finally when she felt they had walked for a long way the Duke knocked on a mahogany door which was opened almost immediately by an elderly maid.

"Good afternoon, Jeannie."

The maid curtseyed and it seemed to Tatika her face lit up at the sight of the Duke.

"I have brought Miss Bray to see my mother," he said.

"Her Grace has been hoping the lady would get here safely," Jeannie said. "Come in, Your Grace."

She opened the door wider and now Tatika saw she was in a large bed-room with a box-window looking out over the garden.

In a big oak fourposter carved and ornamented with many strange devices sat an old lady propped up on lace-edged pillows.

She had white hair, her face was wrinkled, and yet her features were still aristocratic and she must have been exceedingly good-looking in her youth.

She held out a fragile blue-veined hand to the Duke, who raised it to his lips before he said:

"I have brought you Miss Bray, Mama. I rescued her from Torquill who was determined to send her away without your having a chance of meeting her."

"And why should he do that?" the Duchess asked.

Then her eyes flickered over Tatika standing in the doorway.

"No need to answer that question!" she exclaimed. "Come here, Miss Bray."

The Duke stood aside so that Tatika could approach the bed. She curtseyed and the Duchess said:

"You are very young."

"I am not as young as I look, Your Grace," Tatika answered. "I hope you will give me a chance to prove my capabilities."

"You have been in such employment before?" the Duchess enquired.

"She has a most glowing testimonial," the Duke interposed.

"And why should you want to spend your time looking after an old woman?" the Duchess asked.

Despite her age her eyes were shrewd and bright, and Tatika had the feeling they missed very little.

"I am anxious to be in Scotland," she said truthfully.

"Why?" the Duchess asked abruptly.

"Because, Your Grace, it is the most beautiful country I have ever seen," Tatika answered.

"And what other places have you seen?" the Duchess enquired.

"I have travelled quite extensively," Tatika replied, "and what I have seen of Scotland already makes me long to stay here."

"You have a musical voice," the Duchess said unexpectedly. "I cannot stand people reading to me who have voices like corn-crakes, or that last ninny who simpered like some foolish pea-hen."

Tatika laughed.

"I promise Your Grace, that I will not croak at you, nor do I simper."

The Duchess smiled.

"I like you, Miss Bray! I am prepared to risk your leaving me as soon as I have got used to you because you find it too lonely. Are you willing to give the place a trial?"

"I should be very grateful for the opportunity, Your Grace," Tatika said respectfully.

"Then that is settled," the Duke remarked, "although I am afraid, Mama, Torquill will not be pleased with us."

"That will be nothing new!" the Duchess said tartly.

"No indeed," the Duke agreed, "and I think that, as Miss Bray is so anxious to stay in Scotland, together we can brave his wrath."

"Thank you," Tatika said with a relief that seemed to come from her heart.

"Do you think you can be happy here?" the Duke asked.

"I am sure of it," she replied.

His blue eyes met hers. There was an expression in them to which she dared not put a name, and because she felt shy she turned to the Duchess to say hastily:

"If you will excuse me, Your Grace, I would like to wash and change. I have been travelling for two nights. I will not be long, and I could then return to see what I can do for you."

"Do not hurry, Miss Bray," the Duchess said, "Jeannie will find the housemaids who will unpack for you. Tell them if you want a bath."

The Duchess reached out as she spoke and touched a tiny silver bell which lay on the sheet in front of her. The door opened immediately and the maid who had greeted the Duke and Tatika on their arrival stood waiting for instructions.

"Take Miss Bray to her room, Jeannie," the Duchess said. "And have the luggage sent up immediately. Tell the maids to unpack for her."

"Yes, Your Grace."

Tatika curtseyed to the Duchess and then to the Duke. Then with a grace that made her seem as if she glided rather than walked across the room, she followed Jeannie out into the corridor.

Jeannie was a little slow shutting the door, and as

she pulled it to Tatika heard quite clearly the Duchess
say to her son:

"Who is she, and why in Heaven's name should
she wish to come here?"

Tatika found there was little for her to do that
evening. As the Duchess was ill she dined in her bed-
room, waited on by Jeannie and two other housemaids who took the dishes from the footmen who
carried them upstairs.

By the time the Duchess had retired for the
night, Tatika was so tired that she slept peacefully as
soon as her head touched the pillow.

The following day she spent her time trying to
learn what was expected of her and finding that her
duties were certainly not arduous.

She read the newspapers to the Duchess which
were a day old before they arrived, and she found
that Her Grace liked to hear a chapter or two of a
novel, all the latest ones being sent for her approval
from London.

When the Duchess learned that Tatika could
read French she was delighted, and insisted that she
write off immediately for the latest books by Guy de
Maupassant and a number of other French writers.

There were so many books in the Duchess' bed-
room and in her private Sitting-room next door that
there was no reason for Tatika to ask if there was a
Library in the Castle, nor was she able to explore any
further for the first two days after her arrival.

The Duke visited his mother at times when she
was not with the Duchess and she did not see him.

It was on the third afternoon that the Duchess
said after they had finished reading:

"I have only just realised how remiss I have been
in not insisting that you take some exercise. Being old
I forgot that the young must walk and need lots of
fresh air.

"Go out, child, onto the moors in the sunshine,

otherwise I shall have you looking plain and peeky and that I could never abide in a companion."

Her Grace laughed as she spoke and Tatika realised that this was a joke.

She was used by now to the Duchess teasing her and she was well aware that the elderly lady was consumed by curiosity about her background and her reason for taking such employment.

"You are quite sure you do not need me?" Tatika enquired.

"If I want anything, Jeannie will bring it to me," the Duchess replied. "Go for a long walk, and when you come back tell me if you find the loneliness of Scotland insupportable."

"You know I will not tell you that!" Tatika said confidently.

She felt excited at the thought of going outside the Castle and walking freely over the moors.

She was not interested in the formal, rather stereotyped garden with its flower-beds and rose-bushes fighting a continual battle against the winds and the rain.

It was a warm day and Tatika found the breeze was only enough to keep her from feeling too hot as she walked down the tree-bordered drive.

When she reached the great gates with the stone leopards on either side which were part of the heraldic crest of the Strathcraigs, she found that the road ended at the Castle.

Turning north she found a path leading through the fir trees which carried her right out onto the moors.

The path appeared to have been worn by human feet and yet it was narrow and twisting. Tatika followed it through the heather and the rough grass filled with foxgloves and purple thistles, until after she had walked quite a long way from the Castle she came to a burn.

There was not much water in it, but there was a pretty cascade falling over the rocks and filling a pool in which she could see small speckled trout darting around in the sunshine. Then it ran over stones and between heather-covered banks towards the sea.

She could not cross the burn by the cascade, but followed the path up the side of it until above the fall she found to her delight some well placed stepping-stones.

These enabled her to cross with dry feet to the other side where the path continued.

On she walked curious now as to where the path would lead her, climbing all the time between the pine trees and then later rough birchwood, until finally she emerged at the very top of a hill to find beneath her a fantastic view.

She had climbed higher than she realised, and here, where there were several enormous stones as if to mark a special place, she had an unparalleled vista of the sea reaching beyond the bay right out into the ocean towards an endless horizon.

Far below her like a child's toy lay the Castle. Tatika sat down on one of the great stones, smooth and white as if it had been washed by innumerable storms.

She realised she must be on one of the Look-out points used centuries ago by the Scots to watch for the approach of the Vikings.

It was from here the alarm would have been given so that the inhabitants of the Castle, taking with them their women and children, their cattle, their goats and everything valuable they could carry, could slip away far into the hills.

There they would hide in safety until the raiders had collected all they could carry in their ships and returned with their plunder to their own country.

"It is fascinating," Tatika thought, "to imagine the Vikings sailing across the sea in their ships with high pointed bows, their Chief wearing a bronze horned helmet and carrying his shield and long battle-axe."

She felt that moment she was herself a watcher

from the Castle. She could almost hear the shout of warning that would go up to say the Norsemen were approaching.

Then she turned her head from the sea to realise that standing looking at her was the Viking of whom she had been dreaming.

How could he be anything else with his golden hair and vivid blue eyes which seemed to echo the colour of the sea?

His height, the breadth of his shoulders, the very features of his face were all exactly as she had imagined in her dream of the Viking!

"What were you thinking?" he asked in a deep voice.

"I was dreaming that I saw you sailing in from over the sea," she answered without thinking.

"As a Viking," he said with a smile. "Has anyone told you the legend of how the first Magnus came to Castle Craig?"

She shook her head. It now seemed a part of her dream that he should be there and talking to her.

The Duke sat down on another of the great stones so that he was facing her. The two spaniels who accompanied him lay at his feet.

"One of the first great chiefs of the McCraigs," he began, "had a very beautiful second wife. History does not relate her name, but she was reputedly very lovely. He was an old man when he married her, bitterly disappointed that his own son and heir had been killed in battle. They were married, so the legend says for several years, but she did not have a child."

Tatika's hands were folded in her lap and her large dark eyes raised to the Duke's face.

"And then one day," the Duke went on, "the Vikings arrived on a raiding party. The watcher here at the Watch Stones must have given the alarm, and the Chief with his household and everything that was moveable hurried away into the hills, where they hid in the caves that they kept prepared for these frequent emergencies."

"Are the caves still there?" Tatika asked.

"I will show them to you one day," the Duke promised.

"Go on," she begged.

"It was only when they reached safety that they realised the Chief's young wife had been left behind," the Duke said, "but there was nothing that the McCraigs could do about it."

Tatika smiled.

"I think I can guess the rest of the story."

"The name of the Viking Chief was Magnus," the Duke said, "and he stayed a little longer than usual at the Castle while his followers pillaged the country round about."

"And then they went back to Norway?" Tatika asked.

"He said goodbye," the Duke replied, "and I like to think he was unhappy to do so, but he had his duty to his own people. When the McCraigs returned they found the Chief's wife alone and unharmed."

"In the Castle?" Tatika asked.

"Yes, Magnus did not take her with him," the Duke answered. "Perhaps she was not, after all, the woman he really loved, perhaps he had a family waiting for him at home, we do not know."

"Do not spoil the story," Tatika begged. "I am positive they both had broken hearts!"

"They may have had," the Duke conceded, "but in nine month's time the Chief of the McCraigs was presented with a son and heir. The Chief died soon afterwards, so perhaps he never realised that his son grew up looking exactly like his Viking father."

"With fair hair and blue eyes," Tatika said softly.

The duke nodded and continued.

"Every now and then the strain re-appears and another Viking is born. When it happens the child is christened Magnus, as I was."

Tatika gave a little cry of delight.

"It is a lovely story! I was sure, quite sure, the moment I saw you, that you were a Viking!"

"Why are you interested in Vikings?" the Duke asked.

"I have been reading about them in the British Museum," Tatika answered. "And because they were so strong and brave, such a magnificent race of fighting men, I have found myself thinking a great deal about them."

"And dreaming about them?" the Duke asked in his deep voice.

"Yes ... Yes," she answered and felt the colour rising in her cheeks.

"Will you tell me your Christian name?" he asked.

"Tatika."

Even as she spoke she realised she had made a mistake. He had read her reference and would think it strange that Miss Bray—the companion—should have the same very unusual name as her employer's grand-daughter.

"I thought you must be Russian as soon as I saw you," the Duke remarked.

"My mother was Russian," Tatika murmured.

"And from what part of Russia did she come?"

"Novgorod."

"How very strange!" the Duke remarked.

"Why?"

"Because legend, again if it is to be believed, says that in A.D. 862, two years after he came here, Magnus went with the Rus to Novgorod."

"Who were the Rus?" Tatika asked.

"The Scandinavians who were invited to Novgorod by the local population to put an end to their internal feuds."

"And did they?"

"Rurik, whom Magnus served, became the first Prince of Novgorod. The Rus eventually called the whole country Russia.

"How interesting!"

"So perhaps Magnus met your ancestors in Novgorod. What was their name?"

Because she felt hypnotised by the Duke, Tatika told the truth.

"Kaupenski."

"Do you think perhaps we have met before?"

There was a smile on the Duke's lips, but Tatika felt he was speaking seriously.

"In a previous . . . life?"

"Why not? I knew as soon as I saw you . . ."

His voice died away. Tatika's eyes met his and found herself held spellbound.

He was looking deep into her heart, and something seemed to leap into life and draw them to each other so there was no need for words, no need for them to say anything.

For a long long moment they both sat immobile and absolutely still.

Then abruptly as if it was hard for him to do so, the Duke rose to his feet and without speaking, followed by his dogs, he walked away, moving among the trees until Tatika could see him no more.

Chapter Seven

Tatika walked back to the Castle feeling bewildered and unable to formulate her own thoughts.

She only knew it was impossible to forget the expression in the Duke's eyes, and the fact that he was indivisibly linked with her dreams and her thoughts of the Viking Chief.

It was hard to put into words why he had walked away from her without saying goodbye, and yet deep within herself she knew the answer.

She crossed the burn by the stepping-stones and walked back towards the Castle hardly aware of where her feet were carrying her.

She was too intent on her own thoughts to notice anything, until when she had almost reached the stone arch over the front door, she saw someone looking at her from a ground floor window.

It was only a fleeting impression, but it gave her the uncomfortable feeling that she was being watched.

She walked in through the front door. The footmen in their kilts were on duty, and as she moved towards the stairs the Butler, whose name she had learnt was Donald approached her to say:

"Mr. Torquill would speak with you, Miss."

"In his office?" Tatika asked.

"Yes, Miss."

Tatika knew then who had been watching her through the window.

She had not seen Torquill McCraig since he had tried unsuccessfully to turn her away on her arrival and she felt a trifle apprehensive as she went down the corridor and opened the door of the office.

He was not sitting at his desk, but standing in front of the chimney-piece which, Tatika noticed, was like the one in the Chief's Room and of carved stone.

She shut the door behind her and stood just inside the door.

"You wanted to see me, Mr. McCraig?"

"Yes, Miss Bray," he answered. "I wondered where you had been."

"I have been for a walk át the suggestion of Her Grace."

"Quite a long walk! You have been gone over an hour and a half."

"Indeed?" Tatika said quietly. "Her Grace does not require my services until tea-time."

She knew as she spoke that she disliked Torquill McCraig. There was something about him which her instinct told her was wrong with him, quite apart from the fact that he was antagonistic towards her personally.

It was hard to believe that he was a first cousin of the Duke. They were so completely opposite, not only in appearance but also, she was sure, in character.

"Did you see anyone while you were out on the moors?"

The question might sound casual, but Tatika knew that Mr. McCraig was anxious to know the answer.

Quite suddenly she was aware he was dangerous. She deliberately looked puzzled, and then as Mr. McCraig waited she said:

"I think I saw a shepherd as I passed through the

gates. He was a shaggy-bearded man wearing a flat Glengarry bonnet and carrying a long hazel staff."

"Anyone else?"

Tatika did not answer and after a moment Mr. McCraig said:

"Did you see the Duke?"

Tatika frowned a little as if she was concentrating.

"Did he have two dogs with him?" she said.

"I expect so."

"Then that must have been the Duke I saw walking through the woods," she said.

She had the feeling there was an expression of relief on Mr. McCraig's face, but she could not be certain.

"I am glad you enjoyed your walk, Miss Bray," he said. "Are you still intent on remaining in Scotland?"

"I am very happy with the Dowager Duchess, Mr. McCraig," Tatika replied.

Then she curtseyed politely and opening the door left the room.

She knew as she passed through the Hall and up the fine stone staircase that she had left an enemy behind her.

"Why should he be so anxious for me to go away?" she wondered. "And why should he be suspicious that I had seen the Duke?"

She knew intuitively that she must not tell him the truth, and yet she had not told him a direct lie.

It was however an uncomfortable feeling to know that she was being spied on, that her every movement was watched, and that because she had gone for a walk, Torquill McCraig had noted the time she was away from the Castle.

Angie and her friends had been right. There was something sinister here, but Tatika was not yet certain what it was.

She had the feeling that the Duchess and Jeannie were often talking secretly when she entered the room. Their voices would be low, and whatever the subject they were discussing, it was dropped as soon as she appeared.

The following morning as Tatika finished a French novel she had been reading to the Duchess, Her Grace said:

"That is an excellent story and I would like my old friend Lady Berwick to read it. She has been bed-ridden for a year, poor creature, and I often send her a book to help her pass the time."

"I am sure Her Ladyship would enjoy this one," Tatika agreed.

"Then take the book to the office and tell Mr. McCraig to send it to the Countess of Berwick. He knows the address."

"I will do that at once," Tatika smiled, "and then we must choose what I am to read to you next."

She picked up the book, ran along the corridors and down the stairs. She crossed the big Hall, then found that she was moving slower because she disliked the thought of seeing Torquill McCraig again.

She reached the door to the office, but even as she put out her hand towards the handle, she heard voices inside.

"They are in Glasgow," Torquill McCraig was saying, "and they would like to come here as they did last year before their play opens in Edinburgh."

"I do not want them."

There was no mistaking the Duke's deep voice.

"But, Magnus, you found them amusing. The leading lady—what was her name—Angie, is still in the cast."

"I have told you, Torquill, I will not have them here."

"But this is ridiculous, you cannot shut yourself away from all female companionship. Besides we entertained them before, why should you refuse to have them now?"

"I am not prepared to argue, Torquill. This is my house and I will entertain whom I please. If you are so anxious to see again these actresses of whom you speak in such glowing terms, then I am quite certain the Castle will not fall down if you are away for a few days."

"That is not the point, as you well know," Torquill McCraig retorted and his voice was angry. "I am thinking of you."

"And I also am thinking of myself," the Duke replied, "and I will not entertain these women again. Is that clear?"

Tatika realized she was eavesdropping! She only just had time to move away from the door before it opened and the Duke came out of the office.

He turned sharply to the right and therefore did not see her but strode away down the corridor, his kilt swinging as he moved.

She stood watching and she knew that merely the sight of him had the power of making her heart turn over in her breast.

"I am glad, so very glad," she thought to herself, "that he does not wish to see Angie again."

She did not analyse her own feelings, she only knew that a small dark cloud which had hovered at the back of her mind had dispersed, and everything was sunshine.

She opened the door of the office. Torquill McCraig was sitting at his desk and he was scowling.

"What do you want, Miss Bray?" he asked sharply.

"I have brought you this book from Her Grace," Tatika answered and explained where the Duchess wished it to be sent.

Mr. McCraig took the book from her and said abruptly:

"Sit down!"

Tatika looked at him in surprise. She was not used to being spoken to in such a manner. Then she remembered she was only a companion and had no right to resent the discourtesy of her masters.

She sat down slowly on a hard chair which stood in front of the desk.

"When you arrived here," Torquill McCraig began, "I tried to send you back to London, but you insisted on staying. I think it only right that if you intend to remain here you should be warned."

"Warned about what?" Tatika enquired.

"About my cousin—the Duke," Torquill McCraig answered.

Tatika felt herself stiffen. She disliked this man, she did not trust him, and she wondered if he had now discovered that she and the Duke had talked together the previous afternoon.

"You may have heard that a tragedy occurred here three years ago," Torquill McCraig went on.

"I heard someone speak of a tragedy," Tatika said, "but I have no idea what it was."

"The Duchess Irene, my cousin's wife, was strangled," he said harshly.

"Strangled!" Tatika ejaculated.

"She was strangled and thrown from a window of the Chief's Room onto the rocks below."

Tatika gasped.

"Who could have done such a thing?"

"That is the question," Torquill McCraig answered. "The last person to see her alive was her husband."

"You mean . . . the Duke?"

Tatika found it hard to say the words.

"The Duke left the Chief's Room having had a quarrel with his wife. Their voices raised in argument were over-heard quite clearly by the footmen on duty."

Torquill McCraig paused a moment, then said, his eyes on Tatika's face:

"There are always three footmen on duty in the Hall, and there is no possible way of entering or leaving the Chief's Room except by the stone staircase."

"What happened?" Tatika asked.

"The Duke came from the room, walked down

the staircase and went out into the garden with his dogs. A few moments later, Jeannie and a footman entered the Chief's Room to find the window open and no-one there."

Tatika drew in her breath.

"You are suggesting that the Duke threw his wife from the window?"

"I am suggesting nothing," Torquill McCraig said sharply, "I am only relating what happened."

"Then why was the Duke not charged with murder?" Tatika enquired.

"When the Duchess's body was found dead on the rocks with the marks of a man's fingers on her neck, the Sheriff intended to institute an enquiry," Torquill McCraig replied.

"Was there not enough evidence?" Tatika enquired.

She felt she had to know the answer to her questions. She felt as if it was not she who asked them but someone quite detached, someone whose brain was considering the situation quite unemotionally.

"My cousin would have been arrested," Torquill McCraig said, "had not Jeannie said that she entered the room because she had heard a scream. The footmen could not be certain of having heard anything, but Jeannie was so positive, so unshakeable in her contention that the Sheriff finally pronounced the Duchess's death as one of mis-adventure."

"They did not think it was suicide?" Tatika asked.

There was almost a sneer on Torquill McCraig's face as he answered:

"Why should she have committed suicide? She had been very anxious to marry my cousin and she was carrying his child."

Tatika had gone very pale. She wanted to exclaim at the horror of it, to turn aside from the look in Torquill McCraig's eyes which told her he was hoping that she would appear shocked.

With a tremendous effort she held herself

proudly and kept her face quite expressionless as she said:

"I can understand your speaking of it as a tragedy."

"As I have said," Torquill McCraig went on, "it was impossible for anyone else to have entered the Chief's Room. There are in fact only two possible explanations of what happened: either the Duchess fell by accident from one of the windows or the Duke murdered her."

Tatika rose to her feet.

"I am sure, Mr. McCraig, that your loyalty and affection for your cousin make you quite convinced in your own mind that the first explanation is the only valid one."

As she spoke she saw the anger in Torquill McCraig's eyes that she should take his horrific story so calmly.

"It is kind of you to tell me this," Tatika continued, "but I know you would not expect me to be concerned in any way whatsoever with what is entirely a family problem."

She curtsied and went from the room before he could think of a reply and only when she was walking up the staircase again did she find she was trembling.

So this was the sinister secret of the Castle! This was what people gossiped over and discussed in lowered voices.

Now she could understand why the Duke disliked trespassers who stared at him, why he walked alone, why he had withdrawn from the social scene and no longer visited London.

She could imagine what he must feel, having been saved from the hangman's noose only on the word of a faithful maid-servant whose evidence everybody would assume to be prejudiced.

"He did not do it! I know he did not do it!" Tatika said to herself, and reaching the top of the staircase she walked into the Chief's Room.

There was no-one there and she stood looking round.

So many tragedies must have taken place here in the past. It was here for instance that Duke Malcolm had been killed by a treacherous clansman.

Tatika gave a sudden start! Duke Malcolm was perhaps the answer to the present Duke's accusers! She had known, as Torquill McCraig had been talking, that he thought his cousin was guilty.

Duke Malcolm had managed to make himself invisible so that he could mock at the English soldiers from the battlements or from the windows of the Castle, and yet when they entered it they could not find him!

Tatika started to inspect the walls of the Chief's Room, then realised the Duchess would be waiting for her and hurried to Her Grace's apartments.

"Please tell me about Duke Malcolm," she begged as she sat down beside the old lady's bed.

"Who has been telling you about him?" the Duchess enquired.

"The carrier who brought me here from Inverness," Tatika replied. "He told me how the Duke had defied the English soldiers because he could make himself invisible."

"There are hundreds of legends about Duke Malcolm," the Duchess said.

"How was it the English could not catch him?" Tatika asked.

"We have always thought there must have been secret passages in the Castle through which he could pass from one room to another without being seen."

"Has no-one ever found them?" Tatika enquired.

"No-one," the Duchess replied. "The English tried to burn down the Castle in their efforts to find his hiding-place. The children of every generation have continued the search."

She smiled.

"Magnus and Torquill, when they were young, almost pulled the building to pieces in their eagerness to discover how Duke Malcolm could disappear from the battlements without going down the twisting stone staircase which had been guarded by the soldiers."

"There must have been a way," Tatika insisted.

"I only hope you will find it," the Duchess said, "but we had experts here three years ago and they too failed."

There was no need for Tatika to ask why the experts had been asked to the Castle. It was obvious that the Duke had sent for them. He would have been desperate to prove his innocence.

The Duchess was however no longer interested in the past.

"What book are we going to read next?" she asked eagerly, and Tatika forced herself to concentrate on amusing her employer.

When however the Duchess settled herself for a nap after lunch, Tatika was free. She knew that she wanted to think over what had happened that morning, but most of all she wished to see the Duke again.

Putting a small straw hat on her head and tying the ribbons under her chin, she set off for a walk as she had done the afternoon before.

"If Mr. McCraig sees me, I do not care," she told herself. "It is none of his business what I do in my free time."

She was wearing a dress of canary-coloured cotton trimmed with a white collar and cuffs. It was a simple gown but she knew it was exceedingly becoming.

Once she had passed up the drive and found the small path which led to the Watch Stones, she found herself hurrying until she was almost breathless.

But when she came to the place where she had sat the afternoon before looking out to sea, there was no-one there and, although she waited longer than she should have done, the Duke did not come.

Gradually she felt her excitement and elation at the thought of seeing him ebb away from her.

Had she been mistaken in the look she had seen in his eyes? Had the strange magic she had felt within her been personal to herself only?

Why should he think for a moment that his mother's companion, a woman he had been kind enough to champion on her arrival and with whom he had exchanged a few words yesterday afternoon, would be waiting for him again?

"I am being foolish," Tatika told herself and yet she knew there was in fact a link between herself and the Duke which was undeniable.

He was not only the Viking of her dreams, he was a very real man, and she knew there was something between them that could not be explained away.

"Does love really happen like this?" she asked herself.

It was how it had come to her father and her mother. They had seen each other once and that had been enough. Perhaps the right expression was they had found each other!

As far as she and the Duke were concerned, she was certain that he was in fact right and they had known each other in previous lives.

She looked out to sea and said the words aloud that she had whispered in her heart the day before.

"I love you! You are the man I have been waiting for! You are the man I knew I should meet some day to whom I would give my heart!"

It was as if she had planned the whole pattern of her life from the moment she had heard his name at Buckingham Palace! He had been part of her researches at the British Museum and the inevitable outcome to her enquiries at Mrs. Bryant's Domestic Bureau in Mount Street.

It all fitted together like a jig-saw puzzle and now she knew, surely as if the Duke had told her so, that all that was keeping them apart was the question-mark which lay over his wife's death!

"There must be a solution, there must be an explanation," Tatika told herself.

Then shivering a little because she felt lonely and apprehensive, she started to retrace her steps from the Watch Stones back towards the Castle.

She had reached the burn and was seeking the stepping-stones above the cascade, when she saw him coming towards her.

As she stood still looking at him across the burn, the sound of the water seemed somehow like music in her ears and the sunshine was so golden it was almost blinding.

He also stood looking at her with his dogs beside him, leaning on a long hooked staff such as she knew the Chief of a Clan always carried.

Then because she had a wild urgency to speak to him, she hurried across the stepping-stones holding her dress with both hands lest it should touch the water.

He waited for her on the other side.

"I knew you would come to the Watch Stones this afternoon," he said. "I told myself I must not talk to you again and yet in the end I had to come!"

She looked up into his face, and the expression in his eyes told her there was no need for either of them to pretend.

"I wanted to see you," she said simply.

"You know it is impossible! We must not meet!"

"Why . . . not?" Tatika asked.

The Duke did not answer, but she saw the pain twist his lips.

Then as they looked at each other, there was once again that strange magical feeling that drew them by invisible hands until they were close, so close she might in fact have been in his arms.

They stood there utterly spell-bound, until the Duke said with a raw note in his voice:

"You know full well it is impossible! I did not mean to come. Forget that you have seen me."

As he spoke he walked across the stepping-stones and hurried quickly away up the path that Tatika had just descended.

She stood looking after him and felt the tears come into her eyes.

She wanted to run after him, she wanted to beg him to stay, to explain to her why they might not talk, why he was afraid.

She only partially knew the answer. What she could not understand was why he was determined to forgo her companionship and perhaps the companionship of all others.

How could he go through his life in such loneliness, how could he allow the loss even of his wife to affect him in such a manner?

There were so many questions to which Tatika could not find an answer, and as she turned slowly towards the Castle she felt miserably depressed.

For the next ten days Tatika found the Duke had vanished out of her life.

She never saw him except far away in the distance, he never came to visit the Duchess when she was there, she never even heard his voice, and she thought sometimes that she herself would go mad because she longed so desperately to see him.

She lay awake at night thinking about him, praying for him, longing to help him but feeling that the isolation with which he surrounded himself was impossible to pierce.

"I love you! I love you!" she cried into the darkness and knew that her love was hopeless when she could not even speak to him.

She wanted to talk to the Duchess about her son, and here again she came up against a barrier that she could not penetrate.

She sensed the Duchess was deeply upset about the tragedy that had taken place in the Castle, but she was not prepared to talk about it with a stranger.

Although Tatika tried in a dozen different ways to encourage her to talk about the Duke, the older woman was always astute enough to change the conversation or make it impossible for Tatika to ask any more questions.

Only at last did Tatika lower her pride and speak of the Duke to Jeannie.

"I am sure the Duke must have been a very handsome little boy," she said when she had gone to the Sewing Room to take Jeannie a lace handkerchief the Duchess had torn by mistake.

"He was indeed," Jeannie answered, "the most beautiful bairn I have seen in my life! He was like an angel. And his character has always matched his face."

"You are fond of him," Tatika said softly.

"I have loved him ever since the Duchess put him in my arms after he was born," Jeannie answered.

"How upset you must have been at the cruel things that were thought of him when Duchess Irene died," Tatika said daringly.

"Who told you about it?" Jeannie asked fiercely.

"Mr. McCraig," Tatika answered.

"He would do so!" Jeannie said scathingly. "All he thinks about is stepping into His Grace's shoes."

"What do you mean by that?" Tatika asked.

"Mr. Torquill is heir presumptive to the Dukedom."

"That had never occurred to me."

"In my opinion," Jeannie went on, "except for him there would not have been so much fuss made about the marks on Duchess Irene's neck. In fact noone would have noticed them if Mr. Torquill had not drawn attention to the bruises."

"I understand it was you who saved the Duke from being put on trial," Tatika said.

"His Grace never did such a thing, whatever people may say!" Jeannie protested hastily.

"I believe you," Tatika said, "but do people still suspect him?"

Jeannie nodded her head.

"They suspect him right enough. He was not happy in his marriage. Forced on him it was by the Duchess and her friend Lady Berwick."

"Was Duchess Irene the daughter of Lady Berwick?" Tatika said.

"She was," Jeannie said.

"You did not like her, did you?"

"No, I never liked her," Jeannie replied. "She was not the right wife for His Grace."

"Then why did he marry her?"

As soon as Tatika asked the question she knew she had been indiscreet. A blank look came over Jeannie's face and she said:

"All I am telling you, Miss Bray, is that I swore with my hand on the Gospel, and I would swear it again, that His Grace never laid a finger on his wife. If she had marks on her neck, it was not from his hands."

Jeannie would say no more, and Tatika went back to the Duchess.

"Perhaps," Tatika thought to herself, "I am getting fanciful."

But, as she walked around the Castle now knowing its secret, she seemed to sense an atmosphere that she had not noticed at first.

There was something sinister about the great building, about the sea beating on the cliffs below where the Duchess's body had fallen, about the manner in which the Duke never appeared, and the dark glowering face of Torquill McCraig.

She felt herself shivering when she sat alone in the Duchess's private Sitting-room in the evening after Her Grace had retired to bed.

It was then Tatika would hear the wind whistling round the Castle and she thought that sometimes she heard strange voices and even the tramp of marching feet.

"If only Duke Malcolm would come back and tell me his secret," she would whisper to herself.

She had found out from Jeannie about the experts the Duke had brought from Edinburgh to inspect the Chief's Room.

They had even removed the panelling to find out

if there was a secret door hidden behind it. They had climbed up the wide chimney thinking there might be a chamber concealed in it.

They had examined the floor-boards to see if there was a trap-door through which a person could enter or leave the room unseen.

But they had gone away convinced there was no possible entrance to the Chief's Room except through the door which faced the top of the staircase and which was in full sight of the footmen on duty in the Hall.

"They said no-one could have entered without being seen, and the only person who left the room was the Duke himself," Jeannie said.

"There must be an explanation! There must!" Tatika cried.

And yet the more she considered the problem, the more impossible it seemed.

She crept down to the room several times. She examined the big stone chimney place remembering how in Elizabethan homes there were priestholes concealed in the chimney-stack or which could be entered from inside the chimney-breast.

But there did not appear to be anything like that in the Chief's Room, and if the panelling had all been taken off the walls by the experts, what chance was there of her finding a secret passage.

She stood looking at the Claymores and battle-axes on the walls.

Some of them must have been used in the days of Duke Malcolm.

She thought if they could only talk and tell her what to look for, how easy it would be to clear the Duke of the suspicion which she knew was overshadowing him like a dark impenetrable cloud.

She could understand his feelings. She tried to explain to herself why he was avoiding her and why they never seemed to meet accidentally.

She went up to the Watch Stones continually. There she felt that not only she could think more clearly but it was the nearest she could get to the Duke.

It was there he had come to her as the Viking of whom she had been dreaming. It was there, she told herself, that he had recognised for the first time there was something indefinable but infinitival between them.

Tatika came back from the Watch Stones one afternoon in August and realised that the heather was now in full bloom.

The moors were purple, stretching away as far as her eye could see, and the colour was lovelier than she had ever imagined it could be.

When she arrived back in the Castle it was to find the Duchess dressed and in her Sitting-room.

"Oh! I did not know you were going to get up!" Tatika exclaimed excitedly.

"It is about time I took up my duties again," the Duchess replied.

"What duties?" Tatika asked.

"I have to play hostess for my son in the shooting season," the Duchess replied.

"Will there be guests at the Castle?" Tatika asked.

"Yes indeed," the Duchess answered, "but I am afraid you will find them very dull."

Tatika looked surprised and the Duchess went on:

"You must help me to entertain the guests, but they are all elderly people—sportsmen whom my husband used to invite year after year to shoot our moors. As I have said so often to my son, it would break their hearts if they were no longer invited."

Tatika felt her spirits rise. It would be good for the Duke, she thought, to be forced out of his self-imposed isolation.

She was well aware how much the Scottish shooting season meant to a man who enjoyed shooting. Her father talked of it so often.

"If only I were in Scotland!" he would say on an

August or September day when he was working in Vienna or Rome.

"There is nothing more exciting than to shoot at driven grouse," he would tell Tatika when he had been taking part in partridge or pheasant shooting in France, or had been hunting wild boars in Germany.

It seemed to Tatika now that she had been brought up with the idea that shooting grouse was the zenith of every sportsman's ambition.

"Could I go out with the guns one day?" she asked the Duchess.

"I am afraid you would find it very hard walking," the Duchess replied, "and I always have the feeling that women are not really welcome. But I will speak to the Duke and see what he feels about it."

"No, I should not have suggested it!" Tatika exclaimed. "It was impertinent of me, but I remember Papa saying how exciting it was and I thought I would like to see the sportsmen in their butts on the hill side."

"And how could your father afford such an expensive sport?" the Duchess enquired.

Her eyes were inquisitive as they had been so often before. Tatika smiled as she said evasively:

"He had of course many kind friends who invited him as their guest."

"I would have thought," the Duchess said, "that those same kind friends might have looked after you, instead of your having to work for your living."

"Why should they do so?" Tatika answered. "And quite frankly, Your Grace, I am enjoying myself. I am very happy here at the Castle as you well know. In fact I ought to pay you for having me!"

The Duchess laughed.

"You are the most original companion, Miss Bray, I have ever had, and certainly the prettiest."

"I am flattered, Your Grace."

"You need not be," the Duchess replied, "I am speaking the truth. I am just wondering how long it will be before you tell me why you should want to stay in this lonely place without parties, without any amusements, and of course, most important of all, without men."

"I am not interested in men," Tatika said quickly. Then even as she said it she knew it was a lie.

It was however true she was not "interested" in the Duke, she loved him.

She loved him more every time she thought of him, and because the Duchess had said they would be going downstairs to entertain the guests, she felt an irrepressible excitement because she would see him again.

"I want to see him, I want to talk to him, I want to be with him," she told herself.

Then she wondered with a sudden despondency whether after all he had no wish to see her!

Chapter Eight

Every day Tatika found herself getting more and more excited at the thought of going downstairs to dinner in the big Banqueting Hall in the newer part of the Castle.

It was a magnificent room, hung with fine pictures of past Dukes of Strathcraig and their Duchesses, and furnished with a long oak refectory table and side-boards laden with ancient silver vessels.

She had learnt from Jeannie that every evening when the Duke dined, even if he was alone, a piper played the pipes round the table after the last course.

It was the same piper who was personally attached to the Ducal house-hold, and whose piping Tatika heard every morning outside the front of the Castle.

She had seen the man when she looked from the window, splendid in his full dress with his plaid over his shoulder held by a great brooch with a fairngorm in it and a black cock's feather in his cap.

She had found that the music from the pipes gave her a strange elation when they were gay and a sense of melancholy when they were sad.

"What tunes will the piper play at dinner when there is a party?" she asked Jeannie.

"The piper will play the Duke's own music

Salute to Straithcraig," Jeannie replied, "and of course we always have *O'er the Sea to Skye* in memory of Bonnie Prince Charlie."

There was a picture of the unhappy Prince in the Duchess's Sitting-room, and Tatika would think of him hiding in the Castle and how the Scots had suffered untold miseries and even death at the hands of the English through their loyalty to him.

She found that the Duchess also was looking forward to having guests in the Castle, and Tatika suspected that the Dowager was in fact not as ill as she pretended.

"It will be a pleasure," she said once unguardedly, "to have a meal downstairs without having Torquill glowering at me and Magnus looking morose."

As she spoke she must have felt she had been indiscreet, for without waiting for Tatika to reply she quickly changed the subject.

Nevertheless when Tatika went to her own room to change for dinner the night the guests were due to arrive, she felt as excited as a child going to her first party.

Tonight she would see the Duke! There might be little chance of speaking to him, but at least she would be able to look at him at the top of his own table.

It seemed extraordinary that he had managed to avoid her so completely since the day they had spoken together at the cascade.

But the Castle was very large and the Duke's apartments were in a different wing to those of his mother. Tatika could find no real excuse for wandering about the Castle and was forced, except when she went out for a walk, to stay in the Duchess's wing.

But tonight would be different! Tatika stood in front of the wardrobe in her bedroom trying to decide what she would wear.

It would be a mistake for someone in the position of a companion to appear too gorgeously arrayed, and she did not contemplate wearing the very elaborate gowns that she had worn at the Balls during the London Season.

She had finally decided on a dress of *moisseline de soie* which was a very pale mauve, the colour of a Scottish thistle.

The skirt was draped with gauze which cascaded from a large satin bow at the back into a small train.

The bodice was fitted tightly, revealing her slim figure and the budding maturity of her breasts.

But although her shoulders were uncovered, the gauze was gathered over the tops of her arms making a frame for her white skin and the exquisite perfection of her neck.

Tatika took a great deal of trouble over arranging her hair, and when finally she looked into the glass she prayed that the Duke would find her beautiful.

Her eyes were wide and dark with excitement, and the anticipation of seeing the man she loved had brought a faint colour to her cheeks.

She followed the Duchess down the long corridors and felt her heart beating excitedly.

The Duchess looked very regal in a gown of black and silver lamé, and she wore a magnificent tiara of diamonds besides rope upon rope of valuable pearls.

The guests were to be received in the Chief's Room, and although there were always flowers to make a pleasant contrast to the dark panelling of the walls, tonight the gardeners had excelled themselves.

There were great vases of carnations and lilies, and because there had been a chill wind during the afternoon, there was a fire burning in the great chimney-piece.

The Chief's Room was lit by candles although oil lamps were used in the rest of the Castle. They were large ones in carved and gilt candle-sticks and their light was, Tatika knew, extremely becoming to women.

When she and the Duchess entered the Chief's

Room there was no-one else present, but they had been there only a moment when the Duke came in.

Tatika did not realise that a man could look so devastatingly attractive as the Duke appeared in evening-dress.

There was a jabot of lace at his chin and his kilt jacket with its crested silver buttons gave him an elegance that was indescribable.

The fur sporran and the jewelled skene-dhu in his tartan hose were all, Tatika thought, not only a part of Scottish history, but essentially right for him.

He crossed the room towards them and lifted his mother's hand to his lips.

"It is delightful to see you are well again, Mama."

Then he looked at Tatika and she saw from the expression in his eyes that her hope of his finding her beautiful was not in vain.

She knew it was with an effort that he managed to say:

"And may I also welcome you—Miss Bray?"

"Thank . . . you," Tatika answered in a low voice, feeling as if her voice was somehow constricted in her throat.

"The Marquis of Kinbrace, Your Grace," the Butler announced from the door and the Duchess moved forward with an outstretched hand.

"My Dear Marquis," she exclaimed, "how delightful to see you again!"

The Marquis was a man nearing sixty with white hair, but he was still good-looking and he was certainly not too old to have an eye for a pretty girl.

The manner in which he greeted Tatika when they were introduced told her all too clearly that he found her attractive.

Sir Ronald Sinclair was the next arrival, and then General Sir Rennington Hambury and the Earl of Brora.

Two footmen carried round trays containing glasses of madeira and sherry and Tatika tried to listen to the compliments that were being paid to her rather than watch the Duke as he moved amongst his guests.

It was impossible not to notice him towering above the other men, to watch his fair hair and handsome face and know that as far as she was concerned there was no-one else in the room.

Again the Butler appeared in the door.

"Lord Crowley, Your Grace," he said in a stentorian voice.

Tatika stood still, riveted to the spot on which she was standing, feeling as if she was turned to stone.

Then as Lord Crowley turned from greeting the Duchess he saw her.

For a moment he too was still and then ignoring his host he walked to Tatika's side.

"So this is where you have been hiding, Tatika," he said. "I am delighted that I have been successful in finding you when the police have failed."

"The ... police?"

The words seemed to come only in a whisper from Tatika's lips.

"But of course," he replied. "Do you not realise that you are on the list of 'Missing Persons' and had they found you they would have escorted you back to London in a somewhat ignominious fashion? As it is, I myself will take you home."

"I will not ... come with ... you," Tatika said, looking up into his face, her eyes wide and frightened.

She had forgotten that anyone else was present. She did not perceive that the other guests, realising that something strange and unexpected was taking place, had been surprised into silence.

"You will have no choice," Lord Crowley said firmly.

There was a faint smile on his lips which told her he was enjoying her discomforture.

"You are under age, Tatika," he continued, "and the Law insists that you should be in the care of your natural Guardians. Your father is waiting for you and of course—your Step-mother."

"I will not go ... back," Tatika said again, but her voice was trembling and Lord Crowley knew it.

"Have you forgotten that you are engaged to me?" he asked. "I am looking forward very impatiently, little Tatika, to our marriage."

There was a note in his voice which made Tatika feel he was jeering at her helplessness, mocking her because she was completely in his power.

With a little cry, like that of an animal that has been trapped, she turned and ran away from him across the Chief's Room, out through the door and down the staircase to the Hall.

She did not think where she was going, she only knew blindly that she must escape once again from this man who menaced her and whom she hated.

The front door was open and she went through it to run wildly up the drive holding up her skirts with both hands because they impeded her progress.

When she reached the great iron gates she instinctively turned right and finding the path she had trod so frequently before she sped along it, her satin slippers seeming hardly to touch the ground.

It had been raining fitfully all day and when she reached the stepping-stones she found they were only just showing above the water.

However she managed to cross, and then still hardly realising what she was doing she ran on up the path which led through the fir trees and the heather towards the Watch Stones.

She had not gone far before a sudden scud of rain drenched her to the skin. She could feel the rain on her face, on her bare shoulders and running down her back inside her dress.

But she paid no heed to it any more than she noticed that her wide skirts were caught by the twigs of the heather and the gauze torn not once but a dozen times.

Still she climbed higher and higher and the rain

grew heavier, until it was almost torrential as at last Tatika reached the Watch Stones.

She was panting and breathless at the speed at which she had hurried, and now she flung herself down on the ground beside the great stones and laid her cheek against one of them.

"I must get away," she thought desperately, "I must get somewhere and hide! Hide where he will never find me!"

She had ran away from Lord Crowley before because he had horrified and revolted her, but now she knew that, while the thought of being married to him had been terrifying then, it was far worse now.

Now that she loved the Duke, the very idea of another man touching her or kissing her was impossible to contemplate.

"I hate him! I hate him!" she cried aloud and knew that there were no words in which she could express the shrinking of her whole body, nerves and mind from the man who was pursuing her.

She had not missed the intonation in his voice when he had spoken of her Step-mother. How could Tatika forget that Lady Lynch had threatened she would beat her into insensibility if she offended Lord Crowley.

She was quite certain that was exactly what would happen if she had to return to London with him as her captor.

He might still wish to marry her, but that would not placate her Step-mother's anger at the manner in which she had run away before the party at which the Prince of Wales was to be a guest, and the insult she had offered her future husband.

But being humiliated was unimportant beside the fact that Lord Crowley still desired her and still intended to possess her.

"I must hide!" Tatika told herself again, but with the rain beating down on her naked shoulders she thought despairingly that wherever she went he would find her.

There was something relentless about him, something which told her he would never give up the chase, never cease his pursuit until she was helpless and completely subservient to his will.

"If only I could die!" she thought.

She felt that because she was so cold and wet and utterly miserable she might indeed perish alone here at the Watch Stones, where no-one would find her!

She could not cry even in her misery, she was just numb with the horror and helplessness of it all.

Then as it seemed to her that a darkness enveloped her and she was bereft of hope, she felt someone touch her.

"I thought this was where I would find you," the Duke said gently.

"I cannot go . . . back! I cannot!" Tatika cried wildly, trying to prevent him from raising her to her feet.

"At the moment you could not," he replied, "even if you wished to do so."

Then supporting her against one of the great stones he slipped off his evening-jacket and put it over her shoulders.

"I will not . . . go back to the . . . Castle, I have to . . . hide," Tatika told him in an urgent whisper.

The Duke lifted her up in his arms.

"The burn is in spate," he said. "I managed to cross it, but the water was already up to my knees. For the moment at least, my darling, you are cut off from your pursuers."

Tatika could hardly understand what he was saying. She only knew that the security of his strong arms round her was like reaching Heaven.

She hid her wet face against the soft linen of his shirt and knew that in the few seconds he had been without his jacket he too was soaked to the skin.

She shut her eyes. Somehow she did not want to ask questions. She was wet and cold and frightened, but because the Duke was holding her nothing seemed to matter, nothing seemed of importance.

He carried her in his arms and walked away from the Watch Stones towards the trees into which Tatika had seen him disappearing after the first time they had talked together.

The trees partially sheltered them for a little while, and then once again they were in the open and Tatika could feel the rain beating down on her head and soaking through the jacket she wore over her shoulders.

She thought they were moving uphill, but the Duke's stride did not slacken and she did not wish to ask questions. She just wanted to believe that she was safe because she was in his arms.

He must have walked for nearly half a mile before to Tatika's surprise he put her down on her feet.

Opening her eyes, she found it was nearly dark, but she could see the outline of a large hut or small house outside which they were standing.

"I have to find the key," the Duke said and reaching up over the lintel of the door he discovered what he sought and inserted it into the lock.

He opened the door and drew Tatika inside out of the rain saying:

"Stand still. I will light a candle when I can find one."

She leant against the doorway, exhausted by the rain and realising, now she was no longer close to him, how cold and wet she was.

She could feel the skirts of her evening-gown clinging to her legs and rivulets of rain were running from her hair and down her neck.

She put up her hand to wipe her forehead, and as she did so the Duke lit a match and by its flickering light found some candles.

He lit four, one after another, and now Tatika saw that they were in a large hut fashioned out of logs of wood.

It was furnished with a table, a large leather sofa in front of an open fireplace and two or three comfortable arm chairs.

Tatika stared around her in surprise, and realising that the Duke had set a match to the fire laid in the fireplace she closed the door behind her and moved towards it.

The fire had been skilfully laid with shavings beside dry logs and as the flames quickly flickered into life Tatika held out her trembling hands towards them.

The Duke was still moving about the hut. Now he opened another door with a key which had also been hidden.

Tatika wanted to ask him where they were, but it was hard to speak because her teeth were chattering.

There was a sound of drawers being opened and now the Duke returned with his arms full.

"You must get out of those wet clothes," he said. "I am afraid the only thing I can offer you is a dry shirt and some rugs. There is one of Shetland wool which I feel sure will serve you as a skirt."

She looked at him enquiringly and he said:

"This is a Stalker's hut, where sometimes I wait for horses when the burn is in spate. That is why I keep a change of clothes here. I will tell you about it later but first you must get your wet clothes off. I do not wish you to catch cold."

"And what about . . . you?" Tatika managed to say.

"I will also change but elsewhere," he answered. "Here are two towels with which you can dry yourself."

He put everything he carried down on the sofa beside her. Then he disappeared, closing the door behind him.

Tatika found it difficult at first to undo her gown because her hands were so cold. However she managed it, and when finally she had taken off everything she wore, there was more warmth from the fire and she found it easier to dry herself, even while she was still shivering.

The Duke had given her a shirt of soft linen

which was much too big for her but she rolled back the sleeves. There were three rugs for her to choose from, but the one of Shetland wool was obviously the lightest and softest.

She wrapped it round herself twice, grateful for the warmth, and found the Duke had left her a silk tie which she fastened round her waist as if it was a sash.

She picked up her wet clothes from the floor which was covered with rush matting, and modestly hiding her underclothes under the gown she set them beside the fire.

"Can I come in?" the Duke's voice asked.

"Yes, I am . . . dressed," Tatika answered.

She was rubbing her hair with one of the towels as she spoke and turning she saw that he too was wearing a linen shirt like the one he had given her and another kilt. He had dry stockings on his legs, but no shoes.

He crossed the hut to where there was a second door.

"There is a pantry here," he said, "I hope I shall find us something to drink."

She heard him moving about and wondered if she should join him but while she hesitated he came back with a saucepan in one hand and a whisky bottle in the other.

"I have found some whisky," he said, "but as I feel you may not like the taste of it, I will make you a kind of local Mead which is mostly honey and very pleasant. It is also an excellent remedy for keeping out the cold."

He put down the saucepan as he spoke in the fireplace amongst the ashes which, accumulated from a succession of previous fires, were already beginning to glow red. Then he went back to the pantry and fetched two glasses.

He seemed to be concentrating fiercely on what he was doing and Tatika had the idea that he was deliberately not looking at her.

She sat down on the edge of the sofa and went on drying her hair.

Somehow it seemed impossible that she should be here with him alone, and yet she knew this was the moment for which she had been longing these past weeks when she had not seen him.

"I have good news for you," the Duke said. "I thought we had both forfeited our dinner, but I have found it waiting for us in the pantry."

"Something to ... eat?" Tatika asked, feeling she had no interest in food.

"My Factor has thought for some time that one of the shepherds who lives in this part of the moor has been poaching," the Duke said conversationally. "But though he has called at his croft on several occasions, he has never seen a sign of a salmon! Now I have discovered how MacTavish deceived him."

"And how was that?" Tatika asked, since he obviously expected the question.

"There are three large salmon lying in the pantry!" the Duke replied. "MacTavish must have snatched them from the burn and brought them here. When the coast is clear he will take them down to the harbour where he can always find a buyer."

Tatika said nothing and the Duke went on:

"As soon as the fire ceases to smoke, we will grill steaks, and I promise you I will cook them just as well as the Chef at the Castle."

He looked round at her as he spoke and smiled, and she felt her heart turn over in her breast.

While he had been talking he had added some whisky to the ingredients already in the saucepan and now after stirring the mixture he poured it into two glasses.

"Drink this," he said, putting a glass into Tatika's hand.

She sipped it somewhat apprehensively.

"It is delicious!" she exclaimed in surprise.

"I would have been disappointed if you had not

liked it," the Duke answered. "Drink it all, it will keep you warm."

She drank about a quarter of the glass and felt it like a warm stream running through her body.

She had no longer felt as if her teeth were chattering, she no longer shivered.

"Drink a little more," he urged and finished his own glass.

Tatika obediently drank it up before she said:

"I do not wish to become light-headed."

"You will not be," he answered, "there is more honey in it than whisky. And I cannot allow you to be ill!"

Tatika put down her glass and picked up the towel again to go on rubbing her hair. Already it was nearly dry and it fell over her shoulders dark, silky and glistening with the soft lights from the fire and the candles.

She saw an expression in the Duke's eyes and drew in her breath! But without speaking he rose quickly to his feet and walked into the pantry.

He came back after a minute or two with a plate piled with salmon steaks which he set beside a grid that Tatika saw now was built over the fire for just such a purpose.

"I am afraid we are lamentably short of other courses," the Duke remarked, "but I have found a tin of biscuits."

Having put the salmon steaks on the grid he fetched the tin, opened it and placed it beside Tatika on the sofa.

"This is almost a feast," she said.

"It is the first meal we have ever had together."

"I was so looking . . . forward to . . . tonight."

"So was I," he answered, "and you looked very beautiful in your mauve dress."

There was silence. Then Tatika said nervously:

"I ran away from London . . . because I will not and cannot . . . marry Lord Crowley."

"He is much too old for you," the Duke said.

"He is horrifying, repulsive!" Tatika exclaimed violently. "But he will not leave me alone. He is determined to marry me. And he has the support of my father and Step-mother."

"Your name is not Bray?" the Duke said.

"No," Tatika answered. "I am Tatika Lynch. My father is a Diplomat and he is to be our next Ambassador in Paris."

There was silence until the Duke said:

"You must not marry Lord Crowley if you do not wish to do so."

"I detest him, but he is determined," Tatika replied. "And because he is so rich and important, he has the wholehearted support of my Step-mother."

She drew in her breath.

"Can ... can he really make me ... return with him?"

"I imagine he has not the power to do it personally," the Duke answered, "and I will not let him take you from the Castle. We will consider this carefully, but I suggest, if you agree, that we ask your father to visit us, and then I am certain I can persuade him that you must not be forced to marry anyone for whom you have no liking."

Tatika felt as if the Duke was speaking impersonally.

"He is not interested in me himself," she thought desperately. "He will help me but he does not really want me to stay with him! I mean nothing! I have only imagined that he felt for me in the same way that I felt for him."

The disappointment of it made it impossible for her to speak, and the Duke busying himself with cooking the salmon steaks did not continue the conversation.

When the steaks were ready he put them on plates that he had brought from the pantry and gave Tatika a silver fork with which to eat them.

Because she knew he had taken so much trouble,

she forced herself to eat a little of the fresh fish, which was in fact delicious.

It was however hard to think of anything except the fact that the Duke did not appear to want her.

The Duke prepared more of the mead, in which he assured Tatika there was very little whisky. With it she ate one of the biscuits and then the Duke removed the plates to the pantry.

While he was gone Tatika put her feet up on the sofa and leant back against a cushion.

Physically she was warm and comfortable but her mind was in a tumult. She was thrilled because she was alone with the Duke, and yet agonisingly disappointed because he seemed prepared to let her return to her father.

At least however he did not intend to turn her over to Lord Crowley.

At the same time she could not help feeling that, if she did return to London, her Step-mother, whatever her father might say, would still insist on the marriage.

The Duke came back from the pantry and piled some more logs onto the fire.

It was now pleasantly warm in the small wooden hut, and he drew an arm-chair closer to the fire so that he was facing Tatika and only a few feet away from her.

"Do you feel better?" he asked.

"Much better," she replied shyly.

"I am afraid we have to stay the night here, as it is now too late for me to find my way across the moor to the bridge over the new road which is nearly two miles away. But in the morning, if my servants have not come in search of us, I will walk back and tell the grooms to bring you a horse so that you can ride home. The burn will be quite impassable until the spate subsides."

He spoke lightly and to Tatika his tone was of one speaking to a mere acquaintance.

She glanced at him across the space between

them, her eyes very dark and unhappy in her small face. The Duke was not looking at her but staring at the fire.

"I can only express my deep regret," he said, "that the fact that we will have been here all night will undoubtedly cause a certain amount of talk. Not that it is anything unusual where I am concerned."

He spoke with such a bitter note in his voice that Tatika's mind was diverted from her own problems.

"Are you certain," she asked, "that the experts who came from Edinburgh three years ago really searched the Chief's Room thoroughly? There must be something they have missed."

The Duke raised his head.

"Why should you think that?"

"Because," Tatika replied, "it is obvious that there must be a secret passage if only you could discover it. That is how Duke Malcolm earned the reputation of being invisible, and it is the way someone entered the Chief's Room to murder your wife."

The Duke turned his face towards Tatika, his eyes on hers.

"Are you telling me that you believe I am innocent?" he asked.

"Of course you are!" Tatika said positively. "How could you imagine I would think anything else? It is not possible for a man like you to have done such a thing. But somehow we must find the person who did do it."

He stared at her incredulously. Then he said in a voice she had never heard before.

"Do you know what you are saying? In your heart, in the very depths of your being, do you believe in me?"

"But of course ... I know you could not commit ... murder," Tatika said softly.

He rose from his chair to fall on his knees beside the sofa. He did not touch her, he only looked at her, his face on a level with hers.

"I cannot credit it," he said. "Are you sure you

have heard the whole story? Have you not learnt that there is no other way into the Chief's Room and I was the last person to come from it?"

"I have heard all that," Tatika answered, "and I believe, as I believe in God, that you are completely and absolutely innocent."

Her voice trembled as she spoke because he was so near her, and now he gave a strange inarticulate sound as he reached out his arms.

He held her so close against him that for a moment it was difficult to breathe, and then his lips were on hers and at the touch of his mouth she felt an ecstasy and a wonder she had never known before in her whole life.

Her whole being vibrated to his kiss and as her lips responded to him, as thrill after thrill rippled through her, she knew that this was what she had longed for and yearned to feel.

She felt a flame rise within herself to meet the fire in him, and then they kissed each other wildly and passionately.

It was a rapture and an ecstasy which made it impossible to think, and the wonder and the glory of it was like a paean of music rising towards Heaven.

"You believe in me!" the Duke murmured. "Oh, darling, I love you! I have loved you since the first moment I saw you."

"I love you ... too. I have been ... waiting for you ... thinking of you ... knowing that one day I should ... find you," Tatika whispered.

"My darling, my sweet, my little love!"

The Duke kissed her hair, her eyes, her cheeks, then his lips were against the warm softness of her neck and she felt herself quiver with strange sensations she had never known before.

"I love you! You are mine! You have always been mine since the beginning of time! I have always known deep in my heart you were somewhere in the world if only I could find you."

"I have ... dreamt of you," Tatika answered,

"and then you came to me looking exactly like the Viking ... I thought I had seen ... sailing across the sea."

"I must have met you in Novgorod all those years ago," the Duke said, "and I loved you then as I love you now."

He kissed her frantically. She could feel his heart beating against hers, through the thin shirts which were all that covered them.

"You are so beautiful! So unbelievably beautiful," he cried. "But I thought that, if you knew about me, the wonder in your eyes would turn to contempt, and I was afraid ... desperately afraid."

"How could you imagine that I would not know in my very soul what sort of man you are?" Tatika asked.

"You are my love, my heart, my whole life," the Duke cried.

Then he kissed her again until the walls of the hut spun round her, until she could only lie breathless in his arms, her eyes shining like stars, her lips seeking his, her hands holding on to him as if he might escape her.

Then suddenly he released her and rose to his feet.

"This is madness!" he said harshly. "You know I cannot marry you!"

Tatika felt as though he had dashed a jug of cold water in her face.

"Why ... not?"

"Because," he answered, "I could never face the moment when you would begin to doubt me! When as the years went by and there was no explanation of how my wife died, you would begin to think that perhaps you had been mistaken and that I was in fact a murderer!"

He drew in his breath.

"Do you really think I could stay alive and watch you begin to shrink from me, to suspect me, to wonder if you had been mistaken in your trust?"

"Stop!" Tatika cried. "How can you think such things of me? How can you defame our love by such suspicions?"

He was very still and she went on:

"The love we have for each other is not an ordinary one! It is something so beautiful, so much a part of God, that I will not allow you to debase it by suggesting that we will either of us cease to believe in each other or in everything we hold Holy."

She put out her hand towards him.

"Please . . . come to me."

Almost reluctantly he obeyed her to sit down on the edge of the sofa looking down at her.

"We must fight this . . . together," Tatika whispered.

"But I will not marry you until I am exonerated," the Duke replied. "Do you suppose I am not aware that people whisper about me, that even those close to me think that I killed Irene?"

His voice was raw as he continued:

"Sometimes I think I did it in a moment of aberration, that my hatred for her was translated into action, and that my memory merely repudiates the deed."

"It is not true! It is not true!" Tatika cried. "You are torturing yourself! You could never have done such a thing."

"Oh my sweet," the Duke said in a different tone, "you are so young, so perfect in yourself, you cannot understand the twisted minds and emotions of other human beings."

"I am not concerned with other people . . . only with . . . you," Tatika answered.

She thought for a moment he would kiss her, but then he said:

"Whatever you have heard, I imagine that you will not have been told the full story. The truth is that I married to please my mother and because she was so insistent that I must have an heir."

He drew in his breath.

"It sounds weak and despicable now, but the truth is that I was in love, or thought I was, for some years with a married woman."

He saw the expression in Tatika's eyes and said quickly:

"Oh, my precious, it was nothing like this. I was infatuated with her, and because I was young I thought it was love! Yet at the same time something in my heart told me it was not the real love which you and I have for each other. Something that is so perfect that I cannot even now grasp that it is really mine."

"That is just what I ... feel about ... you," Tatika said softly.

The Duke bent forward and kissed her eyes very gently.

"Do not look at me like that," he begged, "or it will be impossible for me to continue my story. I have to make you understand, to know the truth, the whole truth, of what occurred."

"I want to hear it," Tatika answered. "But at the same time I want you to know that I love you. I love you with my mind ... my body and my ... soul. They all belong to ... you and nothing you can say or do can alter that."

Her words broke the Duke's control and his lips sought hers and they kissed each other with a wild rapture which left them both breathless.

Then he took his arms away from her and stood up to stare looking into the fire as he began:

"My mother and Lady Berwick arranged it all between them. Irene was brought to the Castle to stay and she seemed an attractive girl. My mother reiterated over and over again how much she was in love with me. She certainly appeared to like me, and because it was impossible to extricate myself without a scene, I proposed to her and was accepted."

He paused for a moment before he said:

"It seems incredible now that I was such a fool in not being suspicious when Irene was so insistent that we should be married as quickly as possible. But she had very plausible excuses for the haste, and it was only after we were married I discovered the real reason."

"What was . . . that?" Tatika asked in a low voice.

"That she was having a child by another man," the Duke answered.

Chapter Nine

"But why could she not marry the father of her child?" Tatika asked after a moment's silence.

"He was a married man," the Duke answered, "a groom in her father's employment."

"Oh no!"

The exclamation was a cry as Tatika realised all too clearly what it must have meant to the Duke when he learnt the ugly truth.

"It is a situation," he said in a hard voice, "which many men have faced. But I am not pretending, Tatika, that I was not appalled at the thought of such a child inheriting the Dukedom."

"It might not have been a son," Tatika murmered.

"You have forgotten that under the Scottish law, which is very different from the English," the Duke replied, "if there is no son, a daughter can inherit the title."

Tatika saw sharp lines on his face as he stared into the fire before he continued:

"You will understand now that people had good reason to suspect that I murdered my wife."

"Who knew that the child was not yours?" Tatika asked.

"I told no-one," the Duke answered, "either before Irene died or afterwards, when a post-mortem revealed that she was three months pregnant. But I think she had confided in Torquill."

Tatika felt sure that Torquill McCraig, who was jealous of his cousin, would have done his best to defame the Duke by telling the Dowager Duchess and everyone else what the dead woman had confided to him in secret.

But what was the point in saying so now? Tatika was still for a moment and then she said:

"What you have told me only makes me affirm once again that together we must find the murderer."

For the first time since he had begun speaking the Duke turned his face from the fire towards hers.

"Even after what I have just told you," he asked, "do you still believe in me?"

"Do you really expect me to change my mind so easily?" Tatika asked. "I love you, and believe that you are innocent."

He stood looking at her and the expression in his eyes made her tremble. Then he bent down and kissed her bare feet before he took her in his arms and kissed the softness of her neck as he had done before.

He felt her quiver and he pulled open her shirt to kiss her white shoulder and the little hollow between her breasts.

Until, as Tatika wanted his lips more than she had ever wanted anything in her life, his mouth took possession of her, and she knew again that wild ecstasy which seemed to burn through them both like an all-consuming fire.

"I love you! I love you!" the Duke cried. "You are mine and nothing shall take you away from me."

Then he was kissing her frantically as if he felt they faced a danger which would destroy them.

In the rapture of his kisses Tatika felt that she surrendered to him both her heart and soul and became a part of him.

"I love . . . you . . . I love you!"

It was impossible to know who was speaking. They were one and indivisible.

Much later when they were calmer and lay together on the sofa, the Duke holding Tatika in his arms, she said softly:

"I did not . . . know love was like . . . this."

"Like what, my darling?" the Duke asked.

"So wonderful . . . so wild . . . so exciting!"

Then a thought struck her and raising her head a little from his shoulder she said hesitatingly:

"You are not . . . shocked because you . . . excite me so . . . tremendously?"

The Duke laughed and his arms tightened around her.

"How could you think," he replied, "that I do not want your love! It is a thrill beyond anything I have ever known, a joy I cannot express to realise that you respond to me and that, my precious, I can excite you a little."

"Someone once said to me," Tatika told him, "that I was an Ice-Maiden and that I froze everyone with whom I came in contact."

The Duke kissed her forehead before he replied:

"When we are married I will teach you about love, my darling. I will carry you up to the stars and you will know then that nothing exists except us and our love for each other."

His words made her quiver because she could hear the deep desire in his voice. He lifted her chin and looked down into her eyes.

"I love you," he said. "You are more beautiful than I ever believed a woman could be, but, my darling, I will not marry you and I will not make you mine until this cloud which hangs over me now has been dispersed."

Tatika drew in her breath before she said:

"But I want to fight at your side. I want to be with you! I want to belong to you . . . completely."

"I want you too," the Duke answered. "God, how I want you! But, my darling, I wish my son, when you give me one, to be proud of his father just as he will worship his mother—as I do."

His arms tightened around her, but he did not kiss her. He only said in a very serious voice:

"Will you wait for me, my beloved? Is it too much to ask of you?"

"You know it is not too much," Tatika replied. "But I am ready to be your wife ... or ... someone who loves you so overwhelmingly that ... convention does not matter."

He knew what she was trying to say and his eyes were very tender as he said:

"I adore you, and I know that because we have been together in other lives you are already part of me. You are mine and we shall be one for eternity. But I am doing what is best for you, my beloved, when I say we must wait."

Tatika hid her face against his shoulder. She heard the steely inflexible note in his voice, which told her that, however much she might plead with him, he would not change his mind.

All she wanted was to be with him, to belong to him. Nothing else was of any consequence. But she respected him for taking what she knew in her heart to be the honourable course where she was concerned.

They lay close together covered with rugs through the long hours of the night.

Sometimes the Duke rose and put some more logs on the fire and sometimes the fire within themselves burned so fiercely that Tatika felt that the Duke would lose his self-control and possess her physically so that she could be his as she longed to be.

He kissed her until she lost all sense of place and time, could think of nothing except the wonder of his touch, and remembered nothing but the wild rapture of their need for each other.

Yet the Duke still had himself under control, and

when it grew near to dawn Tatika dozed a little, while he held her close with his lips against her hair.

She awoke with a start because the Duke stirred and rose from the sofa.

"What is it?" Tatika asked.

"I think the servants have come," the Duke replied.

He walked towards the door. Tatika sat up on the sofa buttoning the shirt high at her neck and pulling the rug further over her body, but she need not have worried about her appearance.

The Duke went outside the hut, closing the door behind him. She heard voices but after a moment or two he returned alone.

In one hand he carried a leather case.

"Donald guessed we should come here from the storm last night, and he has brought us clothes so that we can both change before we return to the Castle. Will you take this case into the other room? It is little more than a cupboard, but I think you will find it adequate for what you require."

Tatika rose from the sofa to stand with her bare feet on the rush-matting.

"Must we go ... back?" she asked, her eyes on his face.

"We have to be brave, my darling," he answered.

She knew from the expression in his eyes that like her he felt they had awoken from a wonderful dream, and now they must face reality.

She crossed the hut and found that where the Duke had changed the night before was, in fact, nothing but a large cupboard.

There was a wardrobe, a chest, and on the walls hung guns, game-bags and other sporting necessities.

The Duke stood the case down on the floor and when she was alone Tatika opened it and found that one of the maids had packed a light green silk dress and jacket.

It was not a habit for riding, but the skirt was full and she suspected that the animals on which they would return to the Castle were not horses but the sure-footed little mountain ponies.

It was on these the sportsmen rode over the heather or which carried the game-bags, cartridges, the sandwich luncheon, and other requisites for a day's sport.

Tatika took off the linen shirt the Duke had lent her and the Shetland-rug which had made her a warm and comfortable skirt.

Then she dressed herself and arranged her hair in a small mirror which was hanging on the wall.

It would have been difficult to pack a hat in the case, but there were some green ribbons with which she secured her hair neatly so that it would not blow untidily in the wind.

When she was ready, Tatika opened the door into the outer room to find the fire had been made up again; the sofa had been pulled to one side and there was a table with a white cloth laid for breakfast.

"Good morning, Miss."

It was Donald who spoke to her, his face quite expressionless, as if it was nothing unusual to find his Master and his Mistress's companion had spent the night together in a Stalker's Hut.

"Good morning, Donald," Tatika replied.

As she spoke the Duke came in from outside. He had changed into Highland dress and was wearing a tweed jacket and another kilt complete with sporran.

"Douglas has brought us some breakfast," the Duke said. "After the very small dinner we enjoyed last night, I am certain you will find it as acceptable as I do."

Tatika smiled at him as they sat down at the table to find that Donald had cooked them eggs and bacon. There was hot coffee, toast, marmalade and a big pat of yellow butter.

When he had served them, Donald withdrew and Tatika, looking across the table at the Duke, said softly:

"This still seems part of our magic dream. Can it really be happening?"

"I shall never forget last night," the Duke answered.

"Nor I," Tatika replied.

There was no need to say any more. Their eyes met and she knew without putting it into words that the Duke was recalling how close they had been to each other, and how nothing could have been more wonderful.

Tatika dropped her eyes and then she said in a low voice:

"You will not let ... Lord Crowley take me ... home?"

"I have already promised you that I will not allow him to do anything of the kind," the Duke answered. "When we get back to the Castle we will discuss what is the best way to contact your father. It might be wise to send him a telegram."

There was no chance to say more as Donald appeared, and when they had finished breakfast, their wet clothes from the night before were put into the cases and set on a pony's back.

Tatika went outside to find there was sunshine over the moor, the sky was blue and the air smelt fresh and fragrant after the heavy rains.

The Duke lifted her onto the saddle of one of the ponies, then he mounted another to ride ahead while she followed and behind them came three other ponies.

They could only travel slowly over the thick heather which lay between the hut and the bridge over the burn.

When they reached it, Tatika looked at the dark, peaty water splashing over the rocks and realised that the Duke had indeed been right when he said it formed an impassable barrier for anyone who might have wished to pursue her.

From there, the way down to the Castle was

easy, and as the grey building loomed nearer and nearer, Tatika felt her heart sinking.

She was apprehensive and frightened. Even while she was confident that the Duke would protect her, she shrank from seeing Lord Crowley again. She knew he would try and insist on her accompanying him to London.

They reached the drive and now she and the Duke could ride side by side. He turned his head to smile at her reassuringly.

He looked so incredibly handsome, so attractive with his bonnet on the side of his fair hair, that Tatika found it hard to speak. She could only stare at him, her eyes filled with the love she dare not express in words.

They dismounted at the front door. The Duke took Tatika's arm and together they walked up the stone staircase to the Chief's Room.

It was as if they both knew instinctively without asking, that trouble would be waiting for them there.

They entered the room. The sunshine was pouring in a golden haze through the high windows. But Tatika saw with a sharp restriction of her heart that Lord Crowley was standing at the end of the room in front of the chimney piece.

Beside him was Torquill McCraig and another man she did not recognise.

"So, you have returned!"

There was a clear note of accusation in Lord Crowley's voice.

"Unfortunately we could do so no earlier," the Duke replied. "The burn was in spate and it was completely impossible to reach the Castle in the dark."

It seemed to Tatika as if Lord Crowley was hardly listening to him. Instead he said to her with a glint in his eye that she had seen before:

"I have asked the Sheriff here, Tatika, for a special reason."

"The Sheriff?" Tatika asked questioningly, as the Duke went forward with his hand outstretched.

I am sorry, Colonel McNeil," he said, "I did not recognise you for a moment."

"We have not met for some years, Your Grace," the Sheriff replied. "Lord Crowley has made me a request, which of course I cannot ignore."

"What is that?" the Duke enquired.

Tatika drew in her breath. She knew by the expression on Lord Crowley's face, by that dangerous, unmistakeable glint in his eye, that he had been manoeuvring once again. And whatever he had arranged, it would be to her disadvantage.

"His Lordship has requested, Your Grace," the Sheriff answered, "that I should issue a Court Summons against Miss Tatika Lynch, requiring her to return immediately to London and the guardianship of her father."

Tatika gave a little gasp as he continued:

"I understand that in England the police are already searching for Miss Lynch. In the circumstances it can be arranged that she should travel under the custody of Lord Crowley, who is, I understand, the young lady's future husband."

As the Sheriff finished speaking, there was silence until with a little murmur of fear Tatika turned towards the Duke and put out her hand to hold on to his arm.

She wanted to plead with him to help her. She wanted to beg him to deny the Sheriff's authority, but her voice seemed to be lost in her throat and she knew that, whatever she might say, there was nothing the Duke could do.

Once again Lord Crowley was the victor—he had out-manoeuvred her and now she would have to return with him to London to face her Step-mother.

The Duke covered her hand with his and she felt the warm strength of his fingers.

"I am afraid, Colonel McNeil," the Duke said slowly, "you have been misled. The Court Order that Lord Crowley has asked of you may apply to Miss Tatika Lynch. But such a person does not in fact exist, as she is now my wife, the Duchess of Strath-craig."

Tatika raised her face to stare at the Duke in amazement as Lord Crowley took a step forward to say furiously:

"I do not believe it! This is a trick!"

"Tatika is my wife," the Duke repeated quietly.

Then turning to Tatika he said:

"Will you tell the Sheriff so, my beloved?"

She knew from the pressure of his fingers what he wished her to do, and although she did not understand, obedient to his will she said:

"I am your ... wife."

Her voice sounded very faint and frightened.

Then the Duke said sternly:

"There is nothing you can do, My Lord, and in the circumstances I feel you will of course wish to leave the Castle immediately.

"I do not believe it!" Lord Crowley stormed. "Where have you been married? How is it possible this could have taken place without anyone else's knowledge of the ceremony?"

His voice seemed to ring round the Chief's Room. Then the Sheriff, with a faint smile on his lips, as if he understood exactly what had happened, said:

"I must explain, My Lord, that the Scottish law of marriage is different from the English. If His Grace, the Duke of Strathcraig, was not married before, he is married now and in your presence."

"What do you mean by that?" Lord Crowley asked sharply.

"In Scotland a marriage by Interchange of Consent is completely and absolutely legal," the Sheriff replied. "These two people have confirmed in front of witnesses that they are man and wife and therefore from this moment they are legally and irrevocably married!"

Lord Crowley made an inarticulate sound of sheer unmitigated rage, but the Duke looked only at Tatika.

"You are tired," he said gently. "Tell my mother what has occurred and then rest. I shall look forward to seeing you later in the day, after you have slept."

As he spoke he raised her hand to his lips. Without speaking, without looking again at the furious face of Lord Crowley, Tatika went from the room.

She felt very shy at the idea of telling the Dowager what had happened.

The Duchess was in bed, and Tatika thought there was a slightly quizzical expression in her eyes as she advanced across the room towards her.

Then, hurriedly, because she was embarrassed, Tatika told her the story.

As she finished speaking, the Duchess held out both her hands.

"You are married, my dear child? I cannot tell you how pleased I am!" she cried. "Now perhaps Magnus will be happy again. I am so glad, so very glad! I know of no-one whom I would rather have as a daughter-in-law."

Tatika bent to kiss her and the Duchess said:

"It was all my fault that he passed through such misery. I thought I was doing what was best for him, but I know now I was wrong. I am sure that you will make up to him, my dear, for what he has suffered."

"I will try," Tatika promised.

Then because she was in fact very tired she went to her room and almost as soon as her head touched the pillows she fell asleep.

She was awakened by Jeannie drawing back the curtains.

"Have I been asleep for a long time?" Tatika asked.

"For over five hours, Your Grace," Jeannie replied.

"Five hours!" Tatika exclaimed, "I must get up at once!"

"His Grace is anxious to speak with you before the gentlemen return from shooting," Jeannie answered, "that is what I came to tell you."

"They went out shooting?" Tatika asked in surprise.

She had completely forgotten all the other guests who were staying at the Castle.

"Sport comes first when you are in the Highlands," Jeannie answered with a smile. "But His Grace is impatient to see you."

"Then I must hurry down to him," Tatika said.

There was a bath ready, and Jeannie, instead of sending for the housemaids, helped Tatika herself into one of the pretty and more elaborate gowns she had worn in London.

"While you are downstairs, Your Grace," Jeannie said, "I will have your clothes moved."

"Where to?" Tatika asked.

"The Bride's-room, of course!" Jeannie replied. "It is in the old part of the Castle. It is a tradition that if a Chief's wife sleeps there the first night of their marriage then she'll be happy all the years they are together."

Jeannie must have seen the question in Tatika's eyes, for she added:

"When the Duke married before, Your Grace, the room was being redecorated and the Duchess Irene never slept there."

"Oh, I am glad," Tatika said almost beneath her breath.

She was however so anxious to see the Duke that she did not linger talking to Jeannie although there were many things she wanted to ask her.

Instead she ran down the long corridors by the Duchess's Apartments towards the Chief's Room, and when she entered it was to find the Duke staring out of the window, his dogs beside him.

He turned as she entered and they stood for one moment looking at each other, until with a little cry of happiness Tatika ran across the room to throw herself into his arms.

He held her closely against him before he said:

"It was a very strange marriage for you, my darling—no Bridesmaids, no congregation, no Minister to bless us."

"But we are truly married?" Tatika asked.

"We are married as surely as if the ceremony had taken place in a Cathedral," he answered. "You are my wife, Tatika!"

"That is all I wanted," she answered softly.

"I know," he replied, "but my darling, I shall not claim you as mine until I have proved my innocence."

"Then let us do so, and quickly!" Tatika cried.

"I have thought of that!" the Duke said. "I have already written to Edinburgh for another team of experts to come here as soon as they possibly can. I have told them, if necessary, to pull the whole room to pieces!"

"That is what I wanted you to say."

"But suppose they find nothing?"

There was a sudden note of fear in the Duke's voice and Tatika put her arms round his neck.

"The Russians are supposed to be clairvoyant," she said. "Sometimes in the past I have found that I have strange intuitions about things. Now I am completely sure that we shall find a secret passage here and we shall learn how the murderer entered the room."

As she finished speaking she drew the Duke's head down towards her. His arms tightened around her and their lips met.

It was a long kiss and a passionate one. When the Duke released Tatika, there was a flush in her cheeks and her eyes were shining.

"I love you," she whispered.

"You are not to tempt me!" he said almost roughly. "It is going to be very hard, Tatika, to be married to you and not to make you mine. In fact I wonder if any man, looking at you, could stand the strain of it."

He kissed her again, and as he felt her quiver in his arms, he said:

"The guns will be returning in a very short while

from the hill. Will you forgive me, my darling, if I take the dogs into the garden for a very few minutes. I have had a great deal to do this afternoon and I must also confess to having slept for a short while, so they have been rather neglected."

"But of course," Tatika agreed, "but do not be too long. I want to be with you. I want to hear your voice. I want to keep reminding myself that Lord Crowley has gone and I no longer need to be afraid."

The Duke smiled at her words.

Then as if he could not help himself he once again held her against him and kissed her with a long, lingering kiss, as if he could not bear to let her go.

Resolutely he set her from him and walked towards the door, the dogs jumping up eagerly following him out of the room.

Tatika was alone. She looked around her.

Somewhere in this room was a secret passage, which would not only clear the Duke of the slanders which were whispered against him, but would also lift the dark, menacing cloud from his mind.

She knew how deeply he was suffering and how the defamation of his name struck at his pride, not only for himself, but for his ancestry and the honour of his family.

"I must find it! I must!" Tatika said to herself.

She walked round the room staring at the walls with their dark panelling, at the Claymores and shields hanging above it.

She looked at the floor and at the ceiling.

"Is it possible that the murderer could have swung himself down from above?" she wondered.

Then as she stood holding onto one of the damask-covered sofas she heard a faint sound.

She turned her head towards the chimney-piece.

Wide-eyed she saw one of the carved sides which jutted out into the room open slowly about two feet from the floor and making an aperture which reached to the top of the chimney-piece.

The aperture was narrow but just wide enough to allow a slim person to squeeze through it.

Incredulously, Tatika stared, unable to move, thinking she must be dreaming.

Then a man's foot appeared followed by his leg, and finally into the room stepped Torquill McCraig.

"You have found it!" Tatika exclaimed in delight. "You have found the secret passage, how clever of you!"

But even as she spoke her voice seemed to die away in her throat. There was an expression on Torquill McCraig's face which made her hold her breath with fear.

She was so terrified that her heart seemed to stop beating. Then as she turned to run away he reached out and put his hands round her neck.

It happened so suddenly that for a moment Tatika could not realise what had happened. She would have screamed but she felt his fingers tighten, so it was impossible for her to make a sound.

"This time," he said in a low voice, little above a whisper, "there will be no cry to save Magnus, and he will hang as he should have hanged before!"

"You murdered Duchess Irene," Tatika tried to say.

She was not even certain if she pronounced the words, or whether Torquill McCraig merely realised she was trying to say them.

"Yes, I killed her!" he answered, "as I intend to kill you! Do you really think I would let you deprive me of my inheritance? I warned you, but you would not listen, and now you must die and no-one will doubt this time that Magnus killed you!"

As Tatika thought of the Duke and what her death would mean to him, she tried frantically to escape.

She fought against Torquill McCraig, trying to pull his hands from her throat. But she knew even as she did so that he had a maniacal strength, and she was completely helpless.

Already his fingers were tightening as he glared down at her and she could feel her legs weakening so that they must collapse beneath her.

"Magnus . . . Magnus!" she tried to cry, and knew despairingly that he would hang for her death—for another murder he had not committed, and no-one would find the secret passage once it was closed.

Her thoughts were only of the Duke as she felt everything was going dark and she could no longer see Torquill McCraig's contorted face, or the madness in his eyes.

"Magnus!" she tried to cry, "God help you, my love!"

The darkness was covering her ... it was death ... and she could feel herself beginning to fall!

Suddenly there was the sound of a door opening ... a man's voice loud and imperative ... and the pressure on her neck was no longer there.

"My darling! My precious! Oh God, are you alive?"

Strong arms were holding her very tightly and she was no longer about to die.

Far, far away at the end of a long dark tunnel she could hear someone say:

"Torquill McCraig, I arrest you for the murder of the Duchess Irene and the attempted murder of Duchesss Tatika."

"I killed them! Yes, I killed them! I am to be the Duke! Do you hear? No-one shall prevent me from coming into the title!"

Then a frightened frantic shout of:

"Don't touch me! Don't touch me!"

There was the sound of glass breaking and a shrill scream which seemed to grow fainter and fainter, until as it vanished, the darkness covered Tatika completely and she knew no more....

Tatika could hear voices. They were lowered and she could not understand the words they said. Yet because she recognised one of them she felt something warm and happy stir within her hurt body.

Slowly, very slowly, the memory of all that had happened came filtering back into her mind. Although she was practically unconscious she had known that the Duke carried her from the Chief's Room in his arms.

"Is she dead? For God's sake tell me, will she live!"

She heard the anguish in his voice and she wanted to tell him she was alive, but it was impossible to speak. She felt something wet and cold on her forehead and a fiery spirit was being held to her lips.

"Have you sent for a physician?" she heard the Duke ask.

"A groom is leaving immediately, Your Grace."

"Will she be all right?"

"She will be all right." It was Jeannie who assured him so confidently.

"Tatika, my darling! My precious wife!"

There was so much agony in the Duke's words that with an almost superhuman effort Tatika opened her eyes.

"I am alive," she tried to say, but no sound would come from her lips.

It had however been enough! She had seen the tears of relief on the Duke's face, but she had not been able to tell him that she loved him.

Instead she had vaguely known that she was lying on a bed and that Jeannie had brought her something to drink. It had hurt her throat almost unbearably to swallow but she had managed it.

Then she had felt herself drifting away to a warm, soft darkness when she had known that she need not be afraid.

Now, coming back through layer upon layer of sleep, Tatika knew without being told that everything was all right.

"Let me sit up with her, Your Grace?"

She could hear now what Jeannie was saying.

"No, I will stay here on the sofa. If Her Grace needs anything I will attend to it."

There was no mistaking the Duke's deep, quiet voice.

"Your Grace should rest."

"I shall be resting," the Duke answered, "but I do not feel like sleeping."

"I can understand that! Oh, Your Grace—this is the happiest day of my life! You've been proved innocent, as I always knew you would be. I've known you since you were a wee bairn! How could you have committed such a crime?"

"You have always believed in me, Jeannie," the Duke said gently, "and had it not been for you I might well have been hanged."

He paused, until he said with a note of anguish in his voice:

"The Duchess will be all right, Jeannie? You are sure?"

"Your Grace heard what the doctor said," she replied. "The bruises are but superficial and will fade within a week or so. There will be no damage to her brain, and 'tis only the effect of the shock which matters now."

"She appears to be sleeping peacefully," the Duke said.

"Aye, I gave her some herbs which are far better than the doctor's medicine," Jeannie answered. "Rubbishy stuff his be, and does a body no good!"

"He does not approve of your potions!" the Duke revealed with a touch of amusement in his voice.

"I know that, but I was too quick for him! Her Grace had taken my herbs before he arrived!"

"I am sure you know best," the Duke said simply.

"If Her Grace wakes during the night, I've left a glass of honey and glycerine at the side of the bed," Jeannie said. "Make her drink it, Your Grace. It will soothe her throat and take away the pain of swallowing."

"I will do my best," the Duke answered. "Good night, Jeannie, and thank you more than I can ever say for all you have done for me."

"Good night, Your Grace, and the Lord God bless you both for ever," Jeannie said with a passionate sincerity which held a suspicion of tears behind the words.

Tatika heard the door of the bedroom close. Then she knew by the quickened beating of her heart that the Duke had come to the bedside.

She felt a surging happiness because they were alone together, but for a moment she could only savour the wonder of it, until as he did not move, she opened her eyes to look up at him.

For a moment it was difficult to focus. Now she could see his face, and realised that she was in the bed in the Bride's-room, lying in the great carved four-poster with its embroidered hangings which had stood in the Castle for generations.

"It must be late," Tatika thought, because the Duke was wearing a long robe and the room was dark except for the light of two candles and the flickering flames from a fire.

"You are awake, my darling," he exclaimed softly.

Tatika wanted to answer him, but realised she could not speak.

"I have a drink for you," the Duke said, as if he understood. "Jeannie left it for you to drink when you awoke!"

He took a glass from the bed-side table and very gently slipped his arm beneath Tatika's to lift her a little so he could put the glass to her lips.

Because she knew he wished her to do so, Tatika took a sip of the liquid. For a moment she thought it would not be possible to swallow it. She did so, but it was very painful. The second sip went down more easily and the third hardly hurt at all.

The Duke laid her head back against the pillows.

"My darling, my precious, my little love," he said. "Why could I not have saved you from such a terrible experience?"

"Tell me ... what has ... happened ... since," Tatika whispered. Her voice sounded very unlike her own, hoarse and tremulous, but at least she had managed to speak!

The Duke sat down on the side of the bed and lifting her hand to his lips, he replied:

"I love you! Nothing else is of importance except that I love you! And now I am not afraid to say so."

He saw the happiness in her eyes, but because he knew she wanted an answer to her question, he went on:

"We found the plan of the secret passages in Torquill's desk. Also a diary kept by Duke Malcolm, from which we have learned that the passages were in fact incorporated in the Castle when it was first built."

He saw Tatika was listening and went on:

"But the Duke thought that the openings from the passages into the rooms were too obvious, so long before the Rebellion of '45 he brought craftsmen from Italy to alter them."

The Duke looked towards the chimney-piece as he continued:

"Ostensibly they were adding decorative carving to improve the existing medieval chimney-pieces, but my ancestor made them install new entrances in each room."

The Duke smiled.

"They are brilliantly executed! Even now that I know where they are, it is almost impossible to detect any sign of a door in the stone-work."

Then his tone was harsh as he said:

"Once having discovered the plan, Torquill was in the position of being able to move all over the old part of the Castle without being seen."

His lips tightened.

"I saw him at his desk," the Duke went on, "both

when he strangled Irene and again when he attacked you! On the first occasion he was again at his desk when I returned from my walk!"

He looked down at Tatika and his voice was raw as he said:

"If he had killed you, my dearest dear, I would never have forgiven myself for having left you alone in the Chief's Room."

His eyes rested for a moment on her bruised neck.

"Torquill and I were friends as children," he said. "I had no idea he would yearn so desperately to take my place."

"We ... must ... forget it ..." Tatika whispered.

"I can only remember that I am now free to love you," he answered.

She felt a thrill run through her at the desire in his eyes.

She had never seen him look so young, so care-free. The lines had gone from his face and he was more incredibly handsome, she thought, than even she had remembered him to be.

"The shadows have gone!" he said. "This is no longer a Castle of Fear."

"Why did ... you come ... back?" Tatika managed to ask.

"We are protected by some special Fate," the Duke answered. "Just as I was not meant to die and Jeannie saved me, so you were saved, my precious, as it now seems, by a miracle."

He kissed her hand again before he went on:

"I was half-way down the drive. Torquill would have seen me go and he entered the secret passage when the Sheriff arrived. He had returned because in making out the report of our marriage which he wished to send to Edinburgh, he had omitted to ask if you had any other Christian names besides Tatika."

The Duke's fingers tightened.

"I turned back and brought him into the Castle to speak to you himself. Then when we came into the room we saw you, my darling, being murdered by that fiend!"

"He ... meant to make quite sure that you were ... hanged this time," Tatika whispered.

"I know that," the Duke answered.

"He is ... dead?"

"He died when his body touched the rocks," the Duke replied. "He has been taken to the Kirk, and because he was insane he will be buried in the family vault."

The Duke saw the question in Tatika's eyes.

"The Sheriff will make an announcement tomorrow, saying that he committed suicide after confessing to the murder of the Duchess Irene. There will be no mention of his attack on you. I do not wish you involved."

The Duke drew in his breath.

"But you have been involved, my beloved, and I shall never forget what I felt when I thought that he had killed you and that you were lost to me forever."

Tatika knew by the note in his voice what agony he must have suffered, and her fingers quivered in his.

"It is ... all right ... now," she managed to say.

"The doctor swears, my precious, that while your throat is very bruised and sore, there is no permanent damage. In a day or so you will be able to travel."

"Travel?" Tatika asked.

"I want to take you away on our Honeymoon," the Duke replied. "If we stay here, there will be sightseers coming to look at us and there will be friends who want to talk to us. I thought, if you agreed, that we would take my yacht, which is at Inverness, through the Caledonian Canal and across the sea to Iona."

"Where ... Bonnie Prince Charlie ... hid from the English," Tatika murmured.

"I actually own the Castle where he stayed," the Duke said. There was a light in his eyes as he went on:

"It is very quiet and very lonely, but I shall have you to myself, which is what I want more than anything else in the whole world!"

"I would ... love ... that."

"Oh, my darling, I will be very gentle with you," he said, "but we are married, you are my wife, and it will be difficult not to kiss you, not to hold you close however bruised you may be!"

"I want ... you to ... touch me," Tatika whispered.

"Then get well quickly," the Duke answered.

She saw the fire in his eyes, knew that he was longing for her and his desire sent a little thrill through her.

He looked down at her; her eyes were shining with happiness, although her face was very pale. Her dark hair was flowing over the pillows, her bare arms were very white, and her fingers, small and soft, clung to the Duke's hand.

"I love you!" he said. "God, how I love you! And I swear I will make you happy!"

"I am ... happy!" Tatika declared.

"We have our whole life in front of us," the Duke said, "just as I am sure there are so many lives behind us. Now we can plan for the future, there are no shadows, no unhappiness, and no darkness to make us afraid."

He drew a deep breath as if the burden of the past slid away from him and he felt free and untrammelled.

Then he kissed Tatika's fingers one by one, his lips lingering on the softness of her palm and the little blue veins at her wrist.

"You must sleep, my darling," he said, "I shall be near you on the sofa."

He rose as he spoke, then as he could not help himself he bent down to kiss her cheek.

It was a very light kiss—the kiss of a man who was afraid of hurting something so fragile, so precious that he hardly dare touch it.

Yet at the touch of his lips, Tatika felt herself quiver with a sudden rush of ecstasy, and a flame awakened within her heart.

She looked up at the Duke.

"I . . . am still . . . afraid of . . . something."

He could hardly hear the words.

"What is that, my sweetheart?" he said. "What can make you afraid now?"

"Of being . . . alone in this big . . . bed," Tatika whispered, and was spell-bound by the expression on his face.

"My precious! My adorable little Russian wife!" he said unsteadily, and his lips were on hers.

She knew that he had meant once again to be very gentle but as he felt her respond his kiss became more demanding.

Abruptly he lifted his head.

"Do not tempt me," he pleaded as he had done once before. "I shall hurt you. You have to be very quiet, but it is hard for me to remember that when you drive me mad with your beauty and your love!"

Tatika reached out her arms and put them around his neck.

"I want you . . . to carry me . . . to the . . . stars," she said very softly. "You . . . promised and I cannot . . . wait any . . . longer."

Then with a sound of wonder and triumph, the Duke's mouth was on hers and she knew they were one, indivisible and complete as they had been all down the centuries.

The Viking had come home!

ABOUT THE AUTHOR

BARBARA CARTLAND, the celebrated romantic author, historian, playwright, lecturer, political speaker and television personality, has now written over 150 books. Miss Cartland has had a number of historical books published and several biographical ones, including that of her brother, Major Ronald Cartland, who was the first Member of Parliament to be killed in the War. This book had a Foreword by Sir Winston Churchill.

In private life, Barbara Cartland, who is a Dame of the Order of St. John of Jerusalem, has fought for better conditions and salaries for Midwives and Nurses. As President of the Royal College of Midwives (Hertfordshire Branch), she has been invested with the first Badge of Office ever given in Great Britain, which was subscribed to by the Midwives themselves. She has also championed the cause for old people and founded the first Romany Gypsy Camp in the world.

Barbara Cartland is deeply interested in Vitamin Therapy and is President of the British National Association for Health.

Barbara Cartland

The world's bestselling author of romantic fiction.
Her stories are always captivating tales of intrigue,
adventure and love.

☐	THE BORED BRIDEGROOM	6381	$1.25
☐	JOURNEY TO PARADISE	6383	$1.25
☐	THE PENNILESS PEER	6387	$1.25
☐	NO DARKNESS FOR LOVE	6427	$1.25
☐	THE LITTLE ADVENTURE	6428	$1.25
☐	LESSONS IN LOVE	6431	$1.25
☐	THE DARING DECEPTION	6435	$1.25
☐	CASTLE OF FEAR	8103	$1.25
☐	THE GLITTERING LIGHTS	8104	$1.25
☐	A SWORD TO THE HEART	8105	$1.25
☐	THE KARMA OF LOVE	8106	$1.25
☐	THE MAGNIFICENT MARRIAGE	8166	$1.25
☐	THE RUTHLESS RAKE	8240	$1.25
☐	THE DANGEROUS DANDY	8280	$1.25
☐	THE WICKED MARQUIS	8467	$1.25

Buy them at your local bookseller or use this handy coupon:

Bantam Books, Inc., Dept. BC, 414 East Golf Road, Des Plaines, Ill. 60016

Please send me the books I have checked above. I am enclosing $_____
(please add 35¢ to cover postage and handling). Send check or money order
—no cash or C.O.D.'s please.

Mr/Mrs/Miss_____

Address_____

City_____State/Zip_____

BC—6/75

Please allow three weeks for delivery. This offer expires 9/76.

Bantam Book Catalog

It lists over a thousand money-saving best-sellers originally priced from $3.75 to $15.00 —bestsellers that are yours now for as little as 50¢ to $2.95!

The catalog gives you a great opportunity to build your own private library at huge savings!

So don't delay any longer—send us your name and address and 25¢ (to help defray postage and handling costs).